Heavenly Realm Publishing

Houston, Texas

ISBN—9781944383244 (softcover)

Destruction of True Friendships, *Pamela Buchanan*

This book is printed on acid free paper.

Printed in the United States of America

1. FICTION/ Romance / General / Pamela Buchanan 2. FICTION / Christian / Romance / General / Pamela Buchanan 3. FICTION / FICTION / Romance/ African American & Black / Pamela Buchanan

Published By:
Heavenly Realm Publishing
www.heavenlyrealmpublishing.com
shop.heavenlyrealmpublishing.com
Toll Free: 1-866-216-0696

DESTRUCTION

of

True Friendships

Pamela Buchanan

DESTRUCTION

Of

True Friendships

Interlude

As I drove away doing ninety to nothing, tears rolled down my face. I began to wonder what had just happened and why. Flashing lights passed. Red and blue were all I could see. Frantically I stared into space as I drove to free myself from all the horror I had just left behind. Somebody's son, father, and brother and even somebody's daughter, sister, and mother.

Time had finally caught up with me, my husband, and my best friend. The blood on my hands and clothing tells it all. A broken heart had finally shattered into pieces, causing my mind to react to the hurt that drenched my heart.

I finally arrived at the place we called home; 2389 Victoria Lane. This is where our lives as one were first proclaimed. As the garage door opened and I slid into the darkness, all I could remember was the yelling, screaming, and bickering of male and female voices. I ran into the house not stopping until I reached the shower. I began to wash and scrub my body as the blood and particles rinsed from my flesh. My tears constantly flowing as I screamed, "Why me Lord, why me?!"

I freed myself from the wetness and entered my bedroom. Or as I like to call it, my "Cherry Wood Headquarters." The Ruby red satin sheets and comforter perfectly matched the satin swaged drapes brought to life with gold accessories. A bed fit for royalty within a master bedroom to die for. As my tiresome body became one with my fortress, all I wanted to do was disappear. I could foresee an eternity of grief in my future, and as I turned on the TV, I knew the eternity had just begun.

"Breaking News," said the reporter. A couple were found with multiple gunshot wounds at a nearby hotel in an appeared robbery gone wrong. Police aren't releasing the names of the victims, but we were informed that the female did not survive, and the male is in critical yet stable condition." My head dropped on the pillow as the words from the television echoed through my ears. My never-ending tears continued to roll as I asked myself over and over, "What have you done?" I laid there drifting slowly to sleep struggling to answer the question as it replayed in my mind.

Chapter One

As my body began to relax and my mind was set free, I found myself engulfed in childhood memories. It was a fall morning of 1985. I waited for the big yellow bus to arrive and carry me to the one place I dreaded more than anything else, Master Middle School. Just the thought of the worn-down buildings, never-ending assaults of innocent students, and drug transactions made my body shiver. Walking onto the school campus was like walking into the Walmart distribution center for crack heads and prostitutes.

The doors of the bus opened, and the bus driver greeted, "Good Morning Passion!"

"Good Morning Mrs. Jackson!" I said, with a grin as I snagged a seat right behind her. I was never a child who preferred a surplus of people, so I always searched for a seat near the front of the bus. We arrived at the school and I entered the schoolyard doing a quick scan for my girls. "Where are these sluts," I mumbled to myself, as I continued my search. I couldn't help but smile once I finally saw them; talking and laughing about God knows what or who. There were five of us, Brochelle, Kashara, Tayneshia, Sabrina, and me, Passion. Brochelle was the sneaky quiet one, Kashara was the rowdy one, Tayneshia was the overachiever, Sabrina was the laid back one; until provoked, then there was me, Passion, loyal to a fault.

"Hey P! What's up chick?" Kashara said. P was a nickname my friends gave me since there was another "Passion" at our school.

"Nothing much, what are you sluts up to?"

"What's that supposed to mean, and what a funky greeting!"

Tayneisha smirked, everyone else just laughed.

I forgot to mention how sensitive Tayneisha was, especially with anything I said.

"No harm meant, just felt like calling y'all sluts!" I snarled. As I laughed at my crude humor, I felt something off within the group. "Sabrina, what's wrong with you?" I asked.

"Woke up in a mess of a mood and my momma was tripping about everything this morning," Sabrina sighed.

"Oh, I thought Tay had already gotten on your nerves!" Sabrina and I started to chuckle.

Tay, once again, didn't find it very funny.

"Alright, keep it up, y'all going to be upset when I start hanging with someone else," Tay snapped. Before I could counter her threat with a response, Brochelle, unable to contain her laughter says, "Girl, please! Who is going to put up with you other than us!?"

The bell finally rang for the first period of the day, with this morning, beginning like every other morning for the next year. My friends and I would start a conversation in the schoolyard, continue that conversation at lunch, and recap after school on the telephone, in addition to all the other drama we had witnessed throughout the day. We were tight, we were sisters, we were lip gloss loving 6th grade girls, that thought life would be this simple forever. Little did we know then, how short lived that idea would be.

It was 1986, our seventh-grade year when our little worlds turned upside down. Both Brochelle and Tayneshia became pregnant, and I remember like yesterday when the rumors started. Everyone began questioning me and Sabrina as if just because we were friends, we were in the room when our girls got pregnant. It didn't help that this was during the so-called "Baby Boom," you know, "babies having babies," as the older folks would say. I'll never forget the night Tayneshia finally called me and confirmed her pregnancy.

"Get the phone, you know it is for you!" My mother shouted from the living room.

"Hello, who is this?"

"Hey, P this is Tay."

"Hey, what's up?"

"Are you busy? Need someone to talk to."

"Not really, just looking over Science notes. What's up?"

"Passion, I know you've heard the rumors."

"Yes, I have."

"Well, P it's true. Brochelle and I are pregnant."

"Wow. So, what are you going to do? Have you told your Momma?"

"No, not yet I'm scared."

"Tay, I know we all play around about sex, but I didn't think any of us were having sex!"

"You mean you haven't had sex?" Tay exclaimed, "What about those stories you told? Were you lying?"

"Girl, yes!" I said, realizing now that my friends' stories were true. "My mother would kill me! I just wanted to fit in, so I made things up. I thought you guys were making them up too!"

Tay's voice lowered to a regretful whisper, "I wish my stories were made up."

"So, what are you going to do now?" I asked with genuine concern.

"I don't know yet, I talked to Neiman and he wants to get rid of it."

"Wait. What!? It's Nieman's!? I didn't notice my voice rising higher and higher. "He doesn't even go to our school!"

"P! Calm down before Mrs. Martha hears you!" Tay begged.

"I'm sorry, but dang, what are you going to do?"

"Passion I don't know! Just promise you won't say a word to anybody."

"Tay I won't, it's just between us." I made that promise to my friend, but we both knew with time, her secret would reveal itself.

Ring, Ring! Ring, Ring! The sound of someone's attempt to reach me ripped through my reminiscent fantasies. As I searched blindly for my phone, I ran my hands across my satin sheets, feeling the dampness from the sweat I didn't realize was pouring from my brow. I answered the phone without even looking to see who was calling, "Hello!?" I stated. No response. "HEL-LO!" I said again, aggravation ringing from my voice.

No one responded. Silence on the other end, cold, empty silence. I glanced at the clock, six forty-two p.m. As I held the phone in hand, head pounding, reality set back in. I was no longer in the days of my childhood. I was witnessing the reaction to having the line of destruction crossed. My heart was shattered, my mind was racing, the silenced caller finally disconnected.

Chapter Two

As I lie back down, replaying the events that transpired earlier that day, I struggled to decide what my next move would be. All I wanted to do was close my eyes and pray that this was not happening. Folding up into a fetal position, I began to stare into space, wishing more than ever that I could turn back the hands of time.

After Twisting and turning for what felt like an eternity, I gradually drifted back to sleep. "Oh! How pretty she is," a voice stated. "Looks just like her father!" As I looked around, things came into focus and my brain finally comprehended that I was in a hospital room. There lie Tayneshia and her newborn baby girl. I inched closer to the bed as my mother entered the room behind me.

"Hey Passion, want to hold her?" Tay asked.

"No, I'm scared. She is so little." I said, nervously.

Before I could refuse again, my mother interjected, "Go ahead and hold her, I want you to see what not to have!"

"I know that's right Martha!" Tayneshia's mother quickly cosigned with an Amen.

Sadness covered Tay's face, implying how embarrassed she was to have a baby at the age of 13, without her saying a single word her face said it all. During her 9 months of pregnancy, Tay and I had become closer than ever. Sharing more time and secrets than we had in the past.

When Tay's mother found out she was pregnant, naturally, all hell broke loose. Tay ended up moving to live with her aunt for the remainder of her pregnancy, and I became the Godmother of baby Neisha at the tender age of 13.

Over the next few years, Tay and I continued to grow our friendship, maybe because our other friends had gone their separate ways. We were now seniors in high school, no longer pre-teens, and let my mother tell it, we couldn't be told anything!

I remember one incident in which Tay, and I attended a football game at our local high school. While walking toward the entrance gate of the stadium, we became involved in an altercation with some other girls. Tay and I decided to dress alike, black pants, black turtleneck sweaters, and red roper boots. At that moment, my mama was right, nobody could tell us anything! While walking to the entrance, I felt small drops of water on my back. That day, rain was not in the forecast from what I could remember, but I shrugged it off and kept walking.

Once again, I felt the water but this time it seemed to be an abundance of wetness. When I turned to check things out, I notice 3 girls walking behind us laughing and talking loudly, staring as if they were waiting for a response.

So, naturally, I gave them one. "Excuse me, is there a reason you whores are throwing water on us?"

One of the girls answered, "It might be, and what are you going to do about it?"

Then another one spoke up, "It wasn't meant for you, but since you responded, what's up?"

Then the last girl responded as if she had been waiting for her cue to speak.

"Ask your trampy friend" she snarled, "She knows exactly what this is about!"

Suddenly, the largest girl of the group begins to speak rudely in my direction, "Well to tell you the truth, I don't like you either, you think you all that!"

"So what?! Who gives a lovely fuck!" I shouted without a second thought.

The moment I finished my statement the fight began. Tay and I were in a major quarrel. Hair pulling, scratching, kicking; whatever came to mind. It was at that very moment that I knew Tay had my back and she knew I had hers. From that day forward we were inseparable. We were sisters for life.

Chapter Three

"**B**oom!" "*Boom!*" *I awoke* disoriented, thinking I heard... "Boom!" "Boom!" "Boom!" This time it startled me; I did hear someone knocking on my door. I jumped from the bed and hurried down the hallway. As I reached to open the door, reality stepped in again and I noticed I was naked. "One second" I yelled as I went to grab a robe.

"Who is it," I asked through the door.

"Ma'am, this is Officer Green with the Tenison City Police Department."

I slowly opened the door, "Yes, how can I help you?" I asked seemingly confused, knowing all too well why he was there.

"Mrs. Wilson is it?" Officer Green confirmed.

Avoiding his question, I asked instead, "What do I owe this visit, Sir?"

"Well, Mrs. Wilson, is your husband Derrick Wilson?"

"Yes, is he in jail again?" I asked once again seemingly confused and concerned.

"No Ma'am." Officer Green explained, "he was involved in a robbery at the Shamrock Hotel earlier this evening."

"Oh my God!" I screamed, "Is he hurt?"

"Calm down, calm down." Officer Green pleaded. "He has been hurt but his injuries are not life-threatening. Due to the circumstances of the robbery, we have a limit to the information we can disclose since the suspects are still at large. We currently have no leads and are waiting for your husband to become stable enough to talk so we can get any information he may have regarding his attacker." I nodded with my arms folded tightly across my chest, taking every word in as if it were playing in slow motion. "Would you like me to drive you to the hospital?"

"No, No!" I shouted quickly, "I think I'm ok to drive, just tell me where he is officer."

"He is at the Tenison City Hospital, 6th floor in ICU." I mouthed the words, engraining them in my brain, "Tenison City Hospital, 6th floor ICU." Officer Green continued, "I must make you aware that your husband is under police protection until the suspect is apprehended. Unfortunately, the other victim was not so lucky."

"Other victim? What other victim? Was one of his friends with him or something?" I asked confused.

"Mrs. Wilson I really can't advise you of any details at this time" Officer Green stated sternly.

"Okay, okay officer, I need to get dressed and get to the hospital," anxious to get the officer off my doorstep.

As I slowly shut the door, my legs became weak, and I fell to the floor. Thought after thought racing through my mind. Wondering, how would I react once arriving at the hospital? Should I call his family? Will he remember what happened?

I grabbed the first thing I could find to wear and headed straight to the hospital. I drove slowly as I struggled to gather my thoughts. Question after question paralyzing my brain. How will he react to me? Would he speak up about what happened? The more questions that I pondered the more my anxiety began to grow; hands shaking, heart racing, breathing short and shallow. At one point it felt as though my heart was going to jump right out of my chest. "Breathe, P, Breathe," I reminded myself. As I pulled to a stop sign, I began to visualize the first time I introduced Tayneshia to Derrick.

It was the summer of my sophomore year at Ashton College in Ashworth, Georgia. I was back home for my summer break and Derrick and I had been in a relationship for about a year. We met in the small town of Tenison while I was visiting relatives in Texas. Derrick was still a native of Tenison, so we decided to meet in Garden City to spend some time together. The moment I made it back home that summer, I had to call my girl to let her know I was back in town. Unfortunately, Tayneshia was not able to go to college. She had gotten pregnant a year after High school with her second child and was focused on maintaining the relationship between her and her son's dad.

"Hey, Slut what up!?" I said in my usual playful tone.

"Passion is that you!?" Tay yelled with excitement.

"Yes, it's me! Now, what's on the agenda since your girl is in town for the Summer?"

"It's whatever, let's make something happen, what do you have planned for the day?"

"Well," I felt myself beginning to smile and blush, "Derrick is coming into town since we haven't seen each other since Spring Break."

"So, when do I get to meet the famous Derrick?" Tay asked while sucking her teeth.

"Well, as soon as he gets here, I will bring him by, cool?"

"Yeah, girl! That is fine, P I got to go, Mark is on the other line and you know how he can be when I don't answer the phone."

"Mhm," I stated shaking my head, "I'll see you later."

While waiting on Derrick to arrive, I was entertained by my mother and all the latest gossip of Garden City. I soon became restless from hearing who died, who is pregnant, and why she thought I should come home and go to the community college. Before I knew it, I had dozed into a light sleep and was soon awakened by a wet kiss to the cheek. I turned to see those hazel brown eyes and chestnut complexion. Derrick reminded me of a light-skinned Morris Chestnut. He was 25 years old and the father of one son. Although my mother hated the sight of Derrick because he was a street pharmacist, I truly cared for him and treated his son as my own. I wrapped my arms around his neck to draw him closer, pulling him just enough to lose his balance and fall on top of me. We engaged in a slow passionate kiss, to show how much we missed each other without the presence of words.

"Hey, babe. I missed you," he quietly spoke.

"I missed you too," I uttered through a grin, "I'm glad to finally hold you in my arms."

"So, are you going back with me to Tenison?" Derrick asked.

"I'd love nothing more, but babe, I need to get a job, save money and buy some things for school."

"Babe I got you," Derrick reassured, "I want you to spend this summer with me. I will buy whatever you need. Plus, you know I always send you money so find another excuse!" He laughed. "Plus, my little friend misses you," He said raising his eyebrows.

We both laughed.

As wonderful as our time together was, a part of me could not escape the feeling that Derrick was the kind of guy you just knew was cheating. Since I never had proof or reason to doubt his sincerity, I pushed those thoughts to the side, and our relationship was a show-nuff go!

"Babe," I said with excitement, "there is someone I want you to meet!"

"Who is it, another one of your crazy ass kinfolks?" He asked.

"No, my best friend Tayneshia!"

"Oh okay, I'm cool with that."

"Cool, because I promised her this time, I would let ya'll meet."

"Um Passion, can my little friend spend some time inside your little friend first, so he can get some rest?" Derrick whispered, while nibbling on my ear.

"Well, of course, mommy needs some tender loving care as well, but babe, you know that's not going to happen here. Did you forget who let you in? My mother, right?" I gave him a look reminding him where we were.

"Yes, I know, I know. I almost fainted she was being so nice to me," he chuckled. "Even asked me to try to talk you into coming back home and go to school here. Little does she know I want you to move to Tenison with me?"

"For sure babe, in due time." I reassured him, "I love you boy."

"Not as much as I love you." We sealed it with a kiss.

Later that afternoon, after leaving the hotel, we headed to Tay's house. When we arrived, I noticed Tay looking through her blinds. Being aware of Tay's jealous behaviors, I was looking forward to her comments regarding Derrick. We drove up in his freshly washed and waxed 1994 black Cadillac, sitting on sparkling rims with tinted windows. Once parked, Derrick proceeded to my side, he always opened the door for his Queen.

Knock! Knock! The door opened and Tay sprung forward, giving me the sisterly hug, we always greeted each other with. "OOOOH! Tay look at how much weight you have gained," I yelled.

"You would gain weight if you had 2 kids too," she laughed.

"Oh, Tay I'm sorry this is Derrick." I stated as the two exchanged a handshake.

"Hello! I'm glad to finally meet the one who has made this whore settle down!" Tay said, jokingly.

"Watch it now Tay!" I stated as we all laughed.

That day we sat reminiscing about the good old days. We talked about the plans we had when we were young and gossiped about the people in the neighborhood, we grew up in. I could tell Derrick was uncomfortable hearing us talk about our past lovers and sex partners, so I decided it was time to go. Upon driving away Derrick made a statement that stuck in my head.

"Passion, there's something about your friend I don't like. I can't place my finger on it, but I hope your friendship never influences your decisions about our relationship."

"Babe, I'll never let anyone, or anything influence my love for you. I assure you Tayneshia's life could never be mine." I reassured him, "My values of life are my own!"

I reached over to kiss him to let him know that my sincerity was real, and his love was all I needed!

Chapter Four

"**M**a'am, are you alright?" The gentleman spoke while he was tapping on my car window.

As I shook my head to snap back to reality, I realized I was still sitting at the stop sign a block away from my home. I let the window down and answered the gentleman.

"Yes, Sir, I'm so sorry for holding you up. I am fine. I just received some disturbing news." I said, fighting back the tears.

"Ok, Ma'am. I just noticed you sitting here for about fifteen minutes and thought I should approach just to see if I could be of assistance."

"Thank you so much for being concerned," he nodded and walked away.

After rolling up my window, I took a deep breath and proceeded to my destination. Before arriving at the hospital, I decided to call Derrick's sister to inform her of the news. This call was one that I feared the most. Derrick's sister Sheryl was an FBI Agent, and I am pretty sure she would get to the bottom of everything. Sheryl was divorced with three children, stood 6'0, light skin complexion, and weighed maybe two hundred and thirty- five pounds. She loved her brother and considered him one of the most important people in her world. Sheryl always warned me of Derrick's whorish behaviors, often saying, "I love my brother, but why do you stay if you know he's a cheater and has no desire to change?" This statement always stayed within my head. She was one of the few women I admired, and her words held value within me. About two years ago she caught her husband in bed with another woman when she returned home early from a business trip. This ended not only one of her husband's many rendezvous, but it also ended his marriage. Sheryl was so depressed afterward that Derrick and I did anything we could to help her cope with the hurt. This is how Sheryl and my relationship started. She would listen to my heartache, and I would return the favor. I will never forget the first time I saw Sheryl. She was wearing a t-shirt and jogging pants and had recently graduated from the police academy. For the longest time I thought she was a lesbian until Derrick informed me that she was married. Sheryl admitted when she met me that she did not think our relationship would last long due to Derrick's past relationships and my demeanor. She went on to support her belief by advising me of Derrick's dating preference of light-skinned women who weigh less than one hundred and thirty-five pounds. See, I am a dark-skinned woman, long black hair, one hundred and seventy-two pound, and standing five-seven in height. As the years went on, Sheryl would often tease Derrick about how a dark-skinned chick of my height and weight had him sprung. She always encouraged me to put my foot down with her brother so he would refrain from his actions. I never forgot a particular summer day in June, the temperature was pushing one hundred degrees and Sheryl invited me to a family Fish Fry at her cousin Jason's'. She didn't know if Derrick would be there since he and Jason didn't always get along. I had just moved to Tenison and did not know the city well enough to get around on my own, so Sheryl scooped me up. When we arrived at Jason's home, we noticed Derrick's car. Sheryl looked puzzled and we both started to laugh.

"I didn't know he had decided to come!" Sheryl said. "Did he tell you he was coming Passion?"

"No, I hadn't heard about it until you called me."

Sheryl and I proceeded to get out of the car and enter the backyard through the side gate. You could have bought Derrick with a penny when he noticed us. He looked as if he had just seen a ghost. He jumped up from the table where he was playing cards and headed straight toward us.

"Sheryl! What are y'all doing here?" He asked.

Sheryl smirked, "I think we're grown women who decided to attend a family function! The real question is why are you here? You and Jason usually don't get along, plus, why wouldn't you bring Passion to meet other members of our family?"

Derrick looked at me with anger and frustration.

"What's wrong with you?" I asked.

"Nothing, nothing man!"

"What's that supposed to mean!" I responded angrily.

"Passion, nothing. Come on sit down!" Derrick replied.

We all proceeded to walk through the backyard while Sheryl spoke to different members of their family, introducing me to a few of them. I couldn't help but notice the looks I was receiving from them, so I quickly sat in a chair not saying a word. At that exact moment, I saw a female approach Derrick and wrap her arms around his neck and began whispering in his ear. She fit his sister's description of his type; around one hundred and thirty pounds, light-skinned complexion, with every bit of it showing through the revealing outfit she wore. Before I could get up, I noticed Sheryl was headed straight over to them, but I reached them first.

"Derrick, what is this shit?" I asked. Instead of him responding, the female did.

"Excuse me, I'm Candice and who might you be?"

"Well, Ms. Candice. I'm Derrick's fiancé!"

Before any other words could be spoken, Derrick jumped up from his seat, grabbed my arm, and escorted me to the front yard. When we arrived in front of the house all hell broke loose. Our arguing began to escalate, leading to physical blows. Before I knew it, I punched him in his left eye.

"Derrick you know you are wrong that's why you got the nerve to pull me around here!" I shouted.

"Derrick, you'd better not hit her back!" Sheryl had walked out the gate right as my fist connected with Derrick's face. She quickly came in between us attempting to de-escalate the situation, but once again, it only escalated. Derrick came from behind Sheryl and picked me up. He headed to his car and put me inside of it while slamming the door after me. As he tried to walk around the car to get into the driver seat, Candice came running up to him.

"Derrick, so what the fuck is this, and what am I supposed to do now? Please explain what is going on here!" She yelled. Derrick never answered her and just got in the car. He started to drive off without saying a word to her or me. While traveling home we argued the whole way there. Once we got inside our apartment, we received a call from Sheryl making sure we made it.

She and Derrick had a conversation over the phone, and I could tell it got intense because his body language and facial expressions displayed nothing but rage.

"Derrick, if you wanted to be with another woman, why would you move Passion here?"

"Sheryl mind your business!" He yelled.

"Ok, I will, but when trouble comes your way don't call me!"

I did not say one word while they were having their conversation. I just focused on packing my things so I could leave. Finally, Derrick noticed what I was doing and quickly hung up on Sheryl.

"What do you think you're doing and where are you going?"

"I'm going back home! I told you before I moved here that you had to be in this all the way."

He grabbed my arm and started trying to hug me.

"Derrick stop! I am' seriously leaving." I pulled away from him and continued gathering my things.

"Passion, I'm sorry. She does not mean anything to me. Please, let's just sit down and talk about this!"

Well, just like a hurting woman in love, I stayed. He had said all the right things at that time to get me to stay. Not only did his words convince me, but he even called his sister back and assured her that he would change. Sheryl assured him that he would because she was going to hold him accountable. This was only the first of many incidents that Sheryl would have to mediate. I knew I had to call her to inform her of Derrick being in the hospital. She should hear it from me rather than anyone else.

"Hello?"

"Sheryl, how are you today?"

"Passion, I'm doing better than I should be. Where are you?" She asked.

"I'm on my way to the hospital." I paused to hear a response to see how she would react.

"I'm already here."

Not the response I was expecting. "Did anyone explain to you what happened?"

"Not really, I only received bits and pieces, but I will update you on what I know. Derrick has been calling your name the entire time I've been here, so hurry Passion!"

Frantically I asked, "So he can talk?"

"Just a little. I understood some of what he is saying, just be careful Passion and get here quickly!"

"Ok, I'm parking right now."

Chapter Five

As *I ran into the hospital,* thoughts of Derrick uttering my name had me fearful that I would soon be exposed. I tried to fix my face so I would not look so obvious as I approached the help desk. "Ma'am, I'm trying to find my husband, Derrick Wilson. Can you please help me?"

"Sure, just a moment!" She said with a warm smile.

As I waited, I noticed myself beginning to tremble.

"Ma'am, may I see some identification?" The nurse asked.

I reached in my purse and provided my driver's license.

"Thank you, Mrs. Wilson, I will call for one of the officers to escort you to the ICU."

I waited anxiously for the officer to arrive, hands and legs still trembling. He finally arrived after what felt like an eternity and checked my ID before escorting me to Derrick's room. The door sprung opened and there sat Sheryl and Aunt Rose. I walked in slowly dreading what to expect. There he lay with tubes running everywhere. They looked like wires running an electrical device. Before I could mumble a word, I could feel my body fighting against gravity and Sheryl's voice was slowly fading. Next thing I know I was awakened by Sheryl's voice and a cold towel on my face.

"Passion, are you ok?" She said with genuine concern.

"Yes, Sheryl, what happened?"

"You fainted, luckily you fell onto the bed instead of the floor."

"I just cannot handle seeing him like this," I cried.

Derrick's face was badly swollen, and his complexion had a tinted red distinction. His body appeared swollen about twenty pounds more.

"Babe, we understand!" His Aunt stated.

I walked close to Derrick and grabbed his hand. I knew he could feel because he flinched while squeezing my hand.

"Sheryl, I thought you said he could speak? He is only squeezing my hands."

"Passion, he is not speaking clearly, but he has been opening his eyes and responding to us by squeezing our hands. Say something to him to let him know it's you."

"Derrick, babe I'm here. Please open your eyes if you can hear me." I was really scared of what he might do and say as his eyes slowly began to open. Tears ran from his eyes as he looked straight at me. He squeezed my hand tighter as he struggled to speak. "Babe, don't talk I just want you to know I'm here." Derrick tried very hard to respond to me, but his words were not clear at all.

"Hush, Baby Brother. In due time you can tell us everything you need to." Sheryl stated.

I walked over to the window with tears rolling down my face only to look back and notice Derrick's eyes following my every move. All I could do was stare back at him and cry. Sheryl watched both of us as though she was reading our actions to solve the case. "Passion, please come outside with me so we can talk." Sheryl and I walked outside the room and down the brightly lit hallway.

"Passion, I spoke with some of the detectives that arrived at the scene and one of them said he remembered a black Maxima leaving the hotel. Could that have, been you?"

"Sheryl, yes it was! I never meant for all this to happen!" I confessed while sobbing.

"What happened?"

"Well, remember when I told you I noticed Tay's cell number on his phone bill? I began to follow him and watch his actions, but Sheryl I promise you I didn't shoot him or her!"

Sheryl's face had a peculiar look as if she didn't believe me. "Then who did?" She asked.

"Sheryl, I don't know! When I arrived at the room, Derrick was on the floor struggling to make it to the door when I pushed it open. I started screaming and Derrick looked up and told me to get out of there right then because someone was coming back. I tried to pull him, but he was too heavy and kept insisting I leave." Sheryl did not break eye contact even to blink as she listened intently to my defense. "As I ran and got in the car," I continued, "I noticed a man running up the sidewalk toward the hotel room, but I drove off in a hurry scared of what might happen to me if I stayed. I saw the police driving past me as I left, but I was too scared of being accused since my clothes were covered in blood from trying to pull Derrick out of the room. After arriving home my only thought was what just happened and why." I felt faint again being that I just recapped that entire night without taking a breath in between.

"So, Passion, what made you go to the hotel in the first place?" She quizzed.

"I received a call from a female saying she was meeting my husband at the Shamrock Hotel and to catch them if I can! So, I got dressed and headed there, not at all expecting to find what I found."

"Passion don't tell anyone else what you have told me. I am going to get one of my partners to do some research. In the meantime, I want you to stay close to me until we resolve this. Let us get back inside before Aunt Rose gets suspicious." I nodded as we headed back to Derricks' room.

Chapter Six

I *gazed out the window long* after Sheryl and Aunt Rose had left, watching the evening sky turn to night. I glanced over my shoulder to see Derrick looking intensely at me. I walked over to the bed and started to speak to him. "Derrick, can you hear me?"

"Yes, Passion."

His unexpected response startled me.

"I'm so sorry Passion! I guess things finally caught up to me." He stated as tears ran down his cheeks. "How long have you known about the affair?"

"Derrick, I knew she liked you when we got married."

"What? What are you talking about P?"

"The day I called Tay and told her you and I had gotten engaged I asked her to be my maid of honor. She began giving all types of excuses as to why I should not get married to you, plus I was also told later that you two hooked up the night before our wedding." I gazed back out of the window as I continued. "My source saw her enter your hotel room and they didn't see her leave until around 5 am." I looked back at Derrick and he just closed his eyes and turned his head in the opposite direction, speechless as I began to sob. "I guess all these years I've waited for you to tell me the statements were false, only to now find that they were true the entire time. Part of me knew it but I just didn't want to believe it." I walked over to the chair in the corner and sat staring at him. It began to rain outside making it even harder for me to focus on anything other than the hurt and pain I was feeling at this very moment. The rain also forced back the memories of my wedding day; Saturday, April 15, 2000. The biggest day of my life. I was going to be Mrs. Derrick Jaquan Wilson! I was the happiest lady on earth despite all I had endured getting to that day.

Knock! Knock!

"Who is it?" I asked.

"It's your maid of honor! Open up!"

"Hey, Tayniesha. Come on in!"

"Oh, girl you look gorgeous. You sure you want to do this? Looking this beautiful, I know there is a better man out there for you!"

We started to laugh. "Tay, Derrick is the best man for me! You shouldn't do that just because your marriage didn't work out!"

"Ok, just making sure you're ready. I've already done this, and it was pure hell!"

Just before I could respond, the door swung open, and there stood my mother.

"Passion, baby you look amazing!"

"Thanks, Mom! I'm so nervous."

"Baby, there is nothing to be nervous about if you love him and he loves you! Now, come on, everyone is waiting for you!"

"Thanks mom, are my brothers ready?" I asked, trembling with excitement.

"Yes! They are waiting on you!"

"Ok, here I come." I had asked all my five brothers to walk me down the aisle. I came from a large family of five boys and two girls, and it has always been a dream of mine to be given away by all my brothers. Each one of them had played a part in who I had become. My father was never around and with me being the baby of the family, they filled his shoes. This was my way of honoring them for always being there for me. I opened the door to see them standing there patiently waiting for their little sister. All dressed in white tuxedos and burgundy accessories to match the decor I had chosen. We all shared a huddle style hug and now it was time for me to make my entrance into the chapel. The doors swung open and there he was. The man I loved stood facing me with those gorgeous hazel eyes dressed in all white. My bridesmaids were dressed in burgundy strapless dresses with glass slipper heels while the groomsmen stood opposite them in white tuxedos and burgundy cummerbunds. The church was filled with white, silver, and burgundy decor and it seemed as though everyone in the city of Tenison had come out to witness this wedding ceremony. As the wedding march began to play and our guests rose to their feet, I slowly walked down the aisle shaking nervously as tears of joy flowed down my perfectly made-up cheeks. Finally, we made it to the altar, and my brothers handed me off to Derrick so we could begin the process of making our separate lives one. I remember repeating our vows and the kiss that melted my heart into pieces. After the preacher stated, "I now pronounce you man and wife."

All I could think about was how I had won the battle of many. That was one of the days in my life in which I truly believed Derrick loved me and only me. During the entire ceremony, he made me feel as if I were his one and only, and that no one could ever take my position. I was his Queen, and he was my King, forever and for always. That night when Derrick and I entered the hotel suite, he carried me over the threshold and gently laid me on the king bed filled with red roses. They were everywhere! He remembered roses were my favorite flower and had the room decorated with hundreds of them. Once my body hit the bed, the escapades began. Derrick unzipped my dress slowly while kissing every part of my body. I slowly removed his tuxedo, admiring every inch of his flawless complexion. Before long we were butt-ass naked sharing exotic kisses as moans of pleasure slipped through our lips. Derrick made me feel that I had died and gone to heaven.

He kissed my breast passionately then he moved slowly down my stomach until his lips gently massaged my clit.

Derrick's tongue bounced back and forth throughout every inch of my vagina. My body could not help but react to all the pleasure Derricks tongue was delivering. I recalled the noises that flowed from my mouth which in turn caused him to moan while pleasing me even more. Finally, Derrick gave me what I had been craving. His magical stick entered my gates, and the explosions began. The hardness of his penis inside of me made me explode in a matter of minutes. Derrick continued with his lovemaking tricks until both of our bodies exploded as one. We were so relaxed and overwhelmed with pleasure that we fell asleep in each other's arms.

"Passion, Passion!" Was all I could hear as I came back to reality. I turned and noticed Derrick's best friend Marlon standing in the hospital room.

Chapter Seven

"Passion, how is he doing?"** Marlon asked. "I received the information on my voicemail from my wife and I came here straight from work. Do you know exactly what happened?"

"Marlon, I don't know anything yet." I lied. "Derrick hasn't said much at all. You should try and see if he responds to you, he can hear you just fine, but his speech is short and low."

"Hey man!" Marlon shouted at Derrick as he touched his arm. Derrick opened his eyes and spoke softly.

"Hey, Marlon."

"How are you feeling?" Marlon asked.

"Sore as hell man." Derrick replied, wincing as he struggled to sit up.

"So, what went down today?"

"Marlon, I honestly don't know. He came out of nowhere." Derrick began to cough while trying to explain. By this time, I had turned to look at the two of them and Marlon noticed the expression on my face. "Derrick why don't we continue the conversation later." I decided to give them their space and go to the cafeteria to grab something to eat. Before I could get out the door Derrick, in a failed attempt to shout, called out my name, "Passion, where are you going? You do not have to leave. Passion, I love you and baby. I'm so sorry!"

I turned and looked at him and started to cry all over again. I had no words this time, so I continued to walk out the door. Once in the hallway, I paused and rested my head against the ICU door. Anxiety took over my body and had me paralyzed in place. I stood there with hopes of hearing more of the conversation between Derrick and Marlon. If I could just hear more of what happened, I could ease my mind of the role I may have played in the incident. Unfortunately, they both were speaking so softly that I was unable to hear a word. Once my body remembered how to function, I proceeded to the cafeteria. I scanned around the bright white open space eyeing nurses and doctors in scrubs and patients slowly walking about with their IV poles. I finally spotted the perfect spot for me to eat and wind down from all the drama I had experienced the past few hours. As I proceeded to the corner spot and sat down to nourish my body, I noticed a picture across the room. It appeared to be two males and a female embracing each other as though they were close friends. It immediately reminded me of how close Derrick, and I had gotten with Marlon and his wife. I remember when I first moved to Tenison. Marlon had come over to the apartment and when he entered, I was cooking fried chicken, mashed potatoes, and corn. Marlon immediately started sniffing the air like a dog awaiting his meal.

"That's what I'm talking about! A woman that can cook and make the house smell like love. Derrick, I think you hit the jackpot for us!" He chuckled.

I met Marlon on several different occasions when I would visit Derrick back when I was in college, and he always struck me as the perfect gentleman. Even after all these years, he still carries himself as such in my eyes. He also lived up to his role as Derrick's best friend. Whenever Derrick would get into trouble, he would always call Marlon. Whether it was to assist him with getting out of a situation or just for moral support. Derrick's aunt often stated that he and Marlon were inseparable ever since they were children. She would even say Marlon would try to steer Derrick down the right path even if it meant causing trouble for himself. Strangely, I believe as the years went by, I had become closer to Marlon than Derrick would have liked. The thought of our closeness brings me to remember the first incident that Marlon had to mediate. It was a Saturday morning and Derrick had decided to wash my car and leave his for me to run my errands. As I was putting groceries in the trunk, I noticed something sticking from under the spare tire, little did I know I would see pictures of my man with another woman. A naked woman: straddling Derrick while he sat smiling with his hands behind his head. I was so upset that I went to the car wash where the men were gathered to do their male bonding. I did not think twice about his friends being there, I just drove intending to share the hurt that I felt and to get answers immediately. I pulled up and got out of the car without even turning the engine off or closing the door behind me. As I approached Derrick, I threw the pictures, hitting him in the face with them. Before Derrick could even respond Marlon jumped between us.

"Passion, don't do that out here!" Marlon stated. "Don't display this for everyone to see! Come on now!"

"Marlon, Move! I'm so tired of Derrick disrespecting me!" I yelled. "Derrick, what is this shit about?"

Derrick did not respond. He just kept wiping the car because everyone was watching now. One of the things Derrick hated most was being embarrassed, but his lack of response only made me angrier. I continued to agitate him, only to have him finally respond just as I wanted him to.

"Passion, take your ass home right now!" Derrick yelled as he grabbed me under my neck.

"No, Derrick! Not until you explain these pictures!"

"Girl, I'm not going to say it no more! Take your ass home!" Derrick stated fiercely.

After he noticed I was not taking no for an answer. He proceeded to grab my arm and drag me to the car. He opened the door and forced me inside as if he did not feel me hitting and kicking him.

Marlon yelled, "Derrick please don't do that! Y'all about to get the laws called up here! Just let me drive Passion home while both of y'all calm down a bit." Derrick threw his hands up in defeat and walked away. Marlon helped me get straightened out in the passenger seat and drove me away from the carwash. He then asked me where I got the pictures from. I explained to Marlon that the pictures were under the spare tire in the trunk of Derrick's car. At this time, I began to cry. "Marlon, what is it about me that Derrick has to cheat? I cook, clean, and God knows I do whatever he asks in the bedroom. Sometimes, I think he is tired of me and doesn't love me anymore."

"Passion, none of those things are true. Derrick is just stupid sometimes. He thinks with his little head instead of his big one. I know for a fact that he loves you and I can bet you right now it's eating him up insides just to know you found those pictures." Marlon continued to advocate for his boy, "Passion I'm going to talk to him later and see where his head is at. Do not give up on my boy yet and know that you've done nothing wrong. Sometimes a man's ego is stroked by our past and I believe those pictures are a part of his past he wasn't ready to let go of."

I was so caught up in the conversation, I didn't notice that we had arrived at my apartment. "Marlon would you like for me to take you home?"

"No, Passion. I'm going to call Stephanie to pick me up." Stephanie was Marlon's girlfriend at the time.

As we waited for her to arrive, we continued to talk about how men and women hold onto our past to feel better about our present and future. These talks made me trust Marlon to help both Derrick and me when these types of situations occur. Derrick had never mentioned any of the conversations Marlon and I had shared, so he became a trusted shoulder to lean on when I could not lean on anyone else.

At this moment I felt a warm touch on my shoulder, once again dragging me back to reality. I looked up only to find that Marlon had joined me in the cafeteria.

"Passion are you ok?" He asked.

"Yes, Marlon. I am just afraid that this could have all been avoided. For the life of me, I'm so confused by it all."

"Why you say that?" Marlon asked confused.

At this point, I had lost my appetite, so we decided to go outside for a walk. As we strolled around the building, I decided to tell Marlon how I found out about Tay and Derrick messing around. "I knew for a long time but decided to keep quiet and pray that Derrick would stop. Unfortunately, he never did. As bad as it may sound, receiving the call this morning wasn't a surprise at all." I explained to Marlon.

"See, I received a call and the person said, catch us if you can!" I informed Marlon how they went on to give me the location in which my husband was, The Shamrock Hotel. I gave him the details of how when I got there and entered the room number that was given, I found Derrick on the floor and Tay across the bed, shot. Marlon did not say a word. "I tried to get Derrick out of the room by dragging him, but he told me to get out of there and go home. He insisted that I got to safety and not to leave home until I heard from him. I did as he said and now, I'm left with so much confusion about what happened." I stopped walking, and faced Marlon, looking him eye to eye. "Do you have any idea of what may have happened in that hotel room?"

"Well, Passion". He said slowly, breaking our eye contact, "Derrick called me this morning and told me he wouldn't be in today until later because he needed to take care of some things. After I didn't hear anything else from him, I got worried and tried to reach him. He did answer and he told me he would call me back because he was in some heat right then. I asked him did he need me, and he said no. He did not call back either, so I left him alone. Then I received a call from Stephanie about thirty minutes ago telling me Derrick had been shot and was in ICU, so here I am, just as lost as everyone else."

"Marlon, I love Derrick, but I can't go on any longer like this. I really think Sheryl believes I had something to do with it all. Marlon, I couldn't hurt any one of them even though they betrayed me from many angles." Marlon began to hug me while the tears streamed down my face. "I always prayed he would stop cheating and learn to love only me." I cried, "but I see now I was wrong." This made Marlon grip me closer and assure me that Derrick's true love was for me. I wish I believed that as much as he did.

Chapter Eight

Marlon and I reentered, and I noticed Tay's mother and other family members in the emergency waiting room. Tay's mother and my eyes connected as I stared over at them. Mrs. Anderson called out to me, "Passion, thank you for coming. I was wondering if anyone had told you!"

Marlon and I looked at each other in dismay. Marlon looked more shocked than I was, and he was eagerly awaiting my response. I did not know what to say at first, but out of frustration I blurted out, "Mrs. Anderson you must not know?"

"Know what?" She asked, confused.

"My husband and Tay were together at the hotel."

"Passion what are you trying to say?"

"Mrs. Anderson Tay and Derrick were messing around! Looks like karma finally caught up with them both!" Marlon hurried up and put his arms around me and escorted me out of the presence of Tay's family.

"Passion come on. Let's go." Marlon and I walked back to Derrick's room. The closer we got the angrier I became. Once inside, I could not even look at Derrick. I was so angry that I did not even notice the officer in the room until he asked Derrick who we were.

"That's my wife and my best friend."

"Oh, ok. Is it ok to talk in front of them?"

"Sure," Derrick replied.

"Well, Derrick after we got you guys out of there. We were able to speak with a couple of people to see if anyone saw anything. We were able to get a lead for the man that ran away and possibly a description of a vehicle seen leaving the scene. Is it ok if I ask your wife some questions?"

"No. I can answer any questions you may have at this time." Derrick said.

"Ok. Well, can you tell me why the description of the vehicle seen leaving the scene matches the description of a car just like your wife's?"

"Yes, officer. My wife was there. She came in right after we were shot. I was not totally out of it, so I advised her to leave for her safety. I didn't want the shooter to return and hurt her as well." While Derrick was explaining, tears began to roll down his face.

"So, Mrs. Wilson was there?"

"Yes, Sir. I was there!"

"So, why were you their ma'am?" The officer directed this question to me instead of Derrick.

"I received a call about my best friend and my husband at the Shamrock Hotel. The caller told me to catch them if I could! So, I went there and found Derrick and Tay shot."

"Do you know who called you?"

"No, Sir. It was a blocked call, and the voice was distorted." By this time Derrick could tell I was getting nervous by the shaking in my voice. So, he spoke up.

"Officer, I can assure you, she had nothing to do with us getting shot! I know who shot me."

"I understand Derrick, but if she was there, she may be able to give us more information."

"Trust me, the guy who shot me will be identified because after he shot us, I shot him back. I believe I hit him in the arm or shoulder so before long, he will be showing up to the hospital himself." Tenison was a small town and Derrick knew whomever he shot would be brought there since it was the only hospital for miles.

"Ok, Mr. Wilson, when you are ready to provide additional information, I will return. For now, Mrs. Wilson, you need to stay close. Please, all of you, stay safe!" The officer insisted.

"Officer, before you leave. Let me put this name in your ear, Curtis Jones."

"And who may this be?" The officer asked Derrick.

"You said, you wanted the man who shot me! Start there."

"Derrick, Curtis Jones! What the hell!" Marlon screamed.

"Marlon, we will talk later," Derrick said. The look he gave Marlon let me know that they both knew exactly why Derrick said this name.

"Ok, Mr. Wilson. I will look into this Curtis Jones and get back to you with what I find."

"Ok, thanks."

The officer left the room and I sat back down in the corner chair; still upset, but even more confused. I wanted to know who the hell was Curtis Jones and what did he have to do with all of this. I sat staring at Derrick wondering why I have put up with this for so many years. Now my best friend was dead, and my husband was lying in a hospital bed with gunshot wounds. For the first time in my life. I can say I am ashamed to be Mrs. Wilson.

"D, what in the hell is going on?" Marlon asked. I could tell Marlon was upset and wanted answers immediately. Derrick started to speak, but quickly looked over at me and hesitated. Marlon was so frustrated he was pacing the floor.

"Passion, what I have to talk to Marlon about, you may not want to hear."

"Derrick, nothing you can say right now will surprise me. Speak! You owe me that much! My heart is shattered into pieces already!"

"Derrick, I'm trying to figure this shit out, but as every minute goes by. I get more confused." Marlon said. "Ok, so you were in the room with Tay and Curtis Jones burst in the room and shot both of you? Why though? You, I can understand, but her? This does not' make sense!" Marlon exclaimed.

"Marlon man. Not now. I will tell you everything in due time. All I will say is when I get out of here, he is going to pay for all of this." Marlon kept insisting on getting information from Derrick, but Derrick was providing nothing more.

"Marlon, P has been through enough today! As I said, we will talk later, man!" Derrick yelled. He was now upset, and his monitors started beeping due to his blood pressure rising. The nurse entered the room to check on him and advised us that we may want to leave and give him time to get some rest. Marlon and I agreed to leave, but not before Marlon assured Derrick they will be talking again very soon. As I was preparing to leave, Derrick requests that I stay behind.

"Passion, please stay. I need you here with me." I turned around and one part of me wanted to run at high speed out the door, but my heart just would not allow me to leave the man whom I loved.

"Marlon, thanks for coming. I am sure Stephanie is waiting for you. I will call you later."

"Ok, Passion. Call us if you need anything".

"Ok, I will. I love you all." I stated. Marlon and I hugged.

Then he proceeded to leave. I turned slowly around with fear in my heart of remaining in a room with a man I no longer desired to be in the company of. How could this be the man I called my husband, the cause of my life's destruction at this very moment.

Chapter Nine

"**P**assion, please come and sit here on the bed next to me."

"Derrick, why should I sit there now? You weren't wanting me near you earlier at the hotel." Even after stating this, I walked closer to the bed and sat on the edge with my back toward him.

"P, look at me!" Derrick commanded. "Babe, I'm so sorry for everything! I know you hear me say this often and may not believe me right now, but I never meant to hurt you. I love you!"

"Well, Derrick if you love me, why cheat so much? Especially, with my best friend."

"Passion, I can't justify why! I have always known you were everything I needed, but the other women just gave me the thrills I thought I needed." Both of us were engulfed in tears and as usual, Derrick was continuously apologizing. His apologies were falling on deaf ears, his words meant nothing to me.

"Passion, please stop ignoring me and hear me out! You need to hear the full story from me now before everything comes out."

"Derrick, I don't think there is anything you can say right now that would make a difference. Have you realized that Tay is dead for whatever reason? Y'all just had to have your cake and eat it too. Wow, but look at what that got y'all. Why couldn't you both just be happy with the people you had? Plus, it is just not the two of you that this has affected, for the life of me! Who is Curtis Jones and what does he have to do with all of this?"

"Passion, I understand everything you're saying, but I can't change things of the past. All I can do is try and make them right going forward. Can you promise me that no matter how the story unfolds, you will not leave me?"

"Derrick, to be honest, I'm tired and I don't know why I've stayed this long." The truth was that I was just afraid to start over with someone new and learn them, but I would never tell him that. It is like my mother always said, "if you have a dog at home no need to try to find a new one. Especially if you already know all of your dog's tricks. After stating this quietly to myself, I turned to see Derick crying, again, but this was the first time I felt that his tears were sincere. To be honest, the sincerity was not even this intense when he lost his mother two years ago. This left me feeling guilty and confused. I guess I was not considering his current feelings and pain. Not only are his nasty secrets about to be revealed, but he was shot as well.

"Derrick, what is it you really want from me?" As these words left my mouth, I remembered the first time I asked him the same question.

I had just finished high school and was visiting my aunt in Tenison. My aunt Sonya had no children and I always liked to go to her house. She was only seven years older than me, so she was the cool fun aunt that everyone liked and visited, especially on Sundays! We would always go to this park where everyone would hang out and have fun. It was more like a car show and a hoochie festival now that I think about it. Every Sunday we would park in the same spot and Derrick would always park in the same area as us. He was a flashy handsome dude that most girls wanted, and for that reason, my aunt made it clear that he was off-limits. She explained to me that he was one of the biggest drug dealers in Tenison and one of the town's biggest whores. One Sunday, I caught Derrick staring at me. I kept trying to ignore the stares, but I was too infatuated with them not to respond. Yes, he was the guy most girls had been with, and no, I was never a fan of light-skinned guys anyway, but he did not give up trying to get my attention and I was glad he was persistent. I recall one day a florist showed up at my aunt's house with a dozen red roses. Before the florist left, I asked him could he tell me who sent them. He gave me a card that went along with the roses. The card read. "You look like you like roses. From your secret admirer (The Yella Bone) from the park." There was no shame in his game! I could not help but laugh as I walked back into my Aunt's living room.

"Aunt Sonya! Guess what? The guy Derrick sent me roses."

"Passion, I told you to stay away from that guy. Plus, how does he know where I stay?"

"I'm not sure! I have never really talked to him." Every day for about a week I received a different gift. Finally, I acted as though I had had enough of the spoiling and I told my aunt the next Sunday in the park that I would step to Derrick. I put on an act in front of my aunt, but I was enjoying all the attention. Sunday finally came around and before we could even get settled in our usual spot, Derrick was already walking up to my side of the car.

"Hi, I'm Derrick!" He grinned.

"Hello, I'm Passion and this is my aunt Sonya!"

"What's up Sonya?" He replied. He spoke to my aunt as if he knew her already. She responded with an attitude as if she knew more about him than she had shared with me. I later found out that Derrick had dated one of her friends and dogged her out bad.

"So, did you get the gifts I sent you little mama?"

"Yes. I did!"

"Did you like them?" He asked.

"Yes, but do you send all the girls' gifts to get what you want? Or maybe you're just a nice guy." I chuckled.

"Hey, little mama no need to be rude. When I see something I like, I go for it."

"Oh, is that right?"

"Yes, that's right!" We both laughed.

"Be honest. What do you want from me?"

"Truthfully, a phone number and just a little conversation for starters. If that is ok with your aunt of course. I'm getting all types of bad vibes from her right now!" By this time, my aunt turned and looked at Derrick. If looks could kill, he would have been dead on sight. At that point, I could not see what my aunt already knew, but I was due to find out. Derrick received what he sought out to get. My phone number and my attention.

"Passion, please stop all that crying. Everything I got today. I deserved it!" He stated.

At this time, I realized I was no longer engulfed in my memories of Tenison Park but sitting next to Derrick on the twin-sized hospital bed.

"Derrick don't flatter yourself. These tears are not about you. It just too much for me to have to continue to live through. I just do not know what to do! I got to get out of here!" I took off out of the door not even giving him a chance to respond.

Chapter Ten

As I ran out the door. I headed down the hallway to the elevator, growing more and more nervous and upset. When the doors opened, I could not help but notice this lady getting off the elevator. Light-skinned complexion, coke bottle figure, and long black wavy hair was all I recall about her. Sheryl's voice came to mind "Derrick has a type." When she looked up at me, it seemed as if she knew exactly who I was. I didn't have a clue who she was, but there was something about her that made my stomach nervous. I wanted to get out of the hospital so badly that I just kept focusing on getting the elevator doors to close immediately. The ride down gave me a moment to try and remember where I could have possibly known the lady from. Once I arrived at my car, I got in, but my thoughts were set on the mystery lady in the elevator. Then it occurred to me, when Derrick and I first got together, she was the girl he had taken to Jason's house for the Fish Fry!

I could not remember her name, but I sure remember her face and attitude. The real question is, why is she visiting Derrick? I proceeded back into the hospital to see if my woman's intuition was correct, and if it was, I needed answers. As I was going through the emergency door, a man was being brought in with a gunshot wound to his arm. I could not help but stare at the man wondering if he could be the one and only Curtis Jones? The fact of the matter is, I had no clue who he was either. As I passed him, I tried not to stare, but I could not help it. I was so focused on getting back to Derrick's room that I took the stairs two at a time instead of waiting for the elevator.

By the time I got to the door of his room, I was so winded from climbing the stairs that I stood outside the door to catch my breath. As I stood there deprived of oxygen, I could hear two voices from inside the room. I pushed the door open just enough to see her sitting next to him on the bed. The lady from the elevator! My heart felt like it dropped out of my chest and onto the floor. I just stood there listening to their conversation. Maybe I would be able to hear answers to what happened today. I heard exactly what I needed to.

"Derrick, what happened after he came in the room?" She asked.

"I don't know. He came from out of nowhere!" He said.

"So, you mean to tell me, I wasn't the only woman outside of your wife? I didn't mind being the other woman, but damn Derrick!"

"Candice, please don't start that shit. You knew what you were dealing with when you got involved!"

Candice! That's right. That is the name I remembered from the Fish Fry. At this point, I am ready to burst into the room, but something kept holding me back.

"Candice, how did Curtis know I was going to be at the hotel? I never even told you I was going to be there."

"I don't know. I kind of figured he was getting suspicious of us, but he hadn't said a word to me about it." Candice stated.

"But I haven't talked to you in a while, so, what's going on!?" Derrick shouted.

The conversation they were having was not giving me the answers I wanted so I entered the room, not saying a word. I strolled over to the other side of the bed and crossed my arms as I exhaled. Candice jumped up and Derrick became speechless.

"So, is this the lady that has your ass laying up in here?"

"Passion, calm down, and let me explain!" Derrick replied. Candice just stood with a smirk on her face, as if I were the one in the wrong.

"So, I guess you never stopped messing with this Bitch huh?"

"That's right! He never stopped fucking with this Bitch!" She chuckled.

The longer I stood there the angrier I got. "Derrick you know what, everything you said earlier was a damn lie. I am kind of glad you got exactly what you deserved today. I'm just sorry that it was Tay and not this Bitch!"

"Passion stop it. Calm down!" Derrick yelled at me. "I do love you and nobody else can say that! She only came here because she was concerned. Candice, you need to stop all of that too, you know we haven't messed around in a while."

Candice continues to aggravate me by laughing and saying little comments. I believe deep down inside she was eating all this up as flattery but at this point, I was not sure if Derrick was telling the truth or not. All I knew is, I wanted her gone immediately.

"Derrick, who's leaving, me or her?" I asked.

Candice looked at Derrick and stated. "You don't have to answer. I will choose for you. I will leave, but Passion, please believe I will be back!" She strolled on out the door as if she were a beauty queen in a pageant looking at me with devilish eyes. It took everything in me to refrain from jumping over the bed and choking the life out of her.

"Oh, Derrick. I heard the conversation before I came in. You make me regret that I was not the one who pulled the trigger to shoot you! I'm so surprised that I don't have HIV or Aids with all the females you've been messing with!"

"Wait a minute Passion! You are going to damn far now! You act like I've been just fucking any and everything."

"What do you call it Derrick? You know what? I think it's just best you shut the fuck up talking to me right now!" I turned to sit down with my hands covering my face. All I could do was cry. My heart felt as though it had been flipped over and over with a hot cooking utensil.

"Passion listen to me, the guy who shot me was Candice's husband. I do not know why, because I hadn't messed with her in a very long time. Curtis and I have always been rivals, even way back in high school, but babe, I have no clue why this happened!"

"So, you have no clue?" I asked dumbfounded.

"Maybe no clue of why Tay was there either I assume! Answer that Derrick?" I shouted. "What's wrong? I would say, cat got your tongue, but we do not know whose cat it is! Derrick, for once in your life be honest! What's wrong with me that you have to cheat?"

"Passion, I keep telling you that there is nothing wrong with you! The issue is me!"

"Well, I hope getting shot helps you!"

By this time, the door swung open and startled us both. In came Sheryl and his aunt Rose.

"Hello again, how is everything going?" Aunt Rose said, as if they didn't just hear all the drama.

"It's going, Auntie!" Derrick responded.

"So, are you feeling better Derrick?" Sheryl asked.

"I'm doing ok despite the circumstances." He said.

"Passion, are you a little better now?" Sheryl asked.

With my arms crossed and staring at Derrick. I did not want to respond. Therefore, I shrugged my shoulders and gave a long sigh.

"Well, Derrick we got to talk," Sheryl continued, "I heard Curtis Jones may have been the shooter, but what I'm confused about is why he shot you and Tay. Candice wasn't in the room, was she?"

"No, Sheryl!" Derrick said.

"No, Sheryl she wasn't in that room, but she sure made her way to this one a minute ago," I said angrily.

"What, Passion?" Aunt Rose yelled.

"Ok, Derrick! Sheryl said. So, Candice comes here now? For what? I thought this would make the case easier to solve, now, I'm seeing it's going to get more complicated."

"Sheryl, it won't be that difficult, because I haven't been messing around with Candice for a while. Plus, Curtis shot me, and I shot him, and he ran away, then someone else entered the room after Passion left and tried to finish the job."

"So, Passion. You sure you had nothing to do with it?" Sheryl asked. Before I could answer, Derrick spoke up for me, "No, Sheryl. It was a man about six feet tall and about two hundred and fifty pounds. I think I know who it may be, but I'm handling it myself."

"Oh so, you Mr. Bad Ass now! Ok, when the doors of a jail cell open, do not call me! Aunt Rose are you ready to go because the more I stay here the more Derrick might make me shoot him!" Sheryl stated.

"Sheryl! Stop that! Derrick, why don't you let your sister help you?" Aunt Rose pleaded.

Derrick just laid there looking at the TV. "Well, since you want to act like a mute now. I guess Sheryl and I will go! Passion, we will check on you later."

"Thanks, Aunt Rose!" Derrick still did not respond so they proceeded out of the room.

"Derrick, since everyone is leaving, I am going to leave this time too. Maybe you need to be alone to think about what you want for real!"

"Passion, maybe you do need to leave, you keep trying too anyway. I can't believe no one is considering the fact that I am the one that got shot today! Everyone in their feelings though, damn shame. Do you want me to ask Marlon to meet you at the house to make sure you get in safe?"

"Nope, I will call him myself when I'm close to the house. You are so concerned about me now? You should have had that same concern when you were on your way to a hotel room with Tay." Rolling my eyes and grabbing my belongings. "Do you need anything before I leave?"

"Passion, I just want you to remember I love you and I'm still your husband."

"Huh, you right about the husband part, but for how long?"

"What's that supposed to mean, P?"

"Hmmm, never mind! Get some rest, Sir." I said sarcastically. I went out the door and proceeded out of the hospital to the car. Once inside, I had to turn on the music to calm my nerves for the ride to the house. Before I could enjoy the music, I needed to call Marlon to ask if he could meet me at the home.

"Hi, Marlon!"

"Yes, Passion. Everything ok?"

"Yes, are you busy?"

"No, what's up?"

"I'm headed home and wanted to know if you can meet me there. I am kind of scared. I don't know if I'm a target now."

"Passion, you know I will, but why do you feel like you could be a target now?"

"Well, I was leaving the hospital earlier and passed Candice on the elevator, so I went back, and we had a few choice words. She eventually left, but not only that, I saw a man in the emergency room, and he had a gunshot wound to the arm. I do not know Curtis Jones, so I don't know if it was him or not, but get this, Sheryl and Aunt Rose came back, and Derrick told them there was another man involved who came in after Curtis and shot them too. It's crazy Marlon!"

"Damn! I see why you would be scared now Passion; I am getting up. I am going to tell Stephanie what's going on now and I'll be right there. Don't go in until I get there!"

"Ok. Thanks so much! Please give Stephanie my love." Once again Marlon answered the call and stepped up to the plate, a true friend.

Chapter Eleven

As I pulled up in our driveway, I noticed Marlon was already there. I used the remote to let up the garage and drove inside. I proceeded to get out of the car as Marlon walked inside the garage to escort me into the house. He closed my car door and asked me to stay put until he checked the house out. I sat patiently listening to make sure everything was ok inside. Marlon returned to retrieve me and as we entered the den, I could not help but hug him. The embrace he returned gave me a sense of comfort.

"Passion, I know Derrick gave you some ideas of what may have happened, but did he ever just tell the real story?"

"No, Marlon! I just heard bits and pieces when I was eavesdropping on his conversation with Candice."

"I just can't understand why he keeps messing with her. She has always been trouble for him since high school."

"Well, my mother always told me that if it causes you trouble and you keep staying there, you must like it."

"Not sure Passion, but we can see Derrick likes trouble." We both laughed.

After talking more with Marlon, I could tell the comfort level I was feeling was becoming more than that of friends.

"Marlon, I have to be honest with you, some feelings are arising within me for you. I have tried to suppress them, but the more I'm in your presence, the harder it's becoming. Please don't look at me funny for confessing my thoughts."

"Passion, what are you saying?"

"Forget it Marlon, with all that's going on, I guess I'm talking out of my head!"

"P, what if I say I'm having the same feelings?" He asked.

"I guess the answer to that is Stephanie!" I turned to look directly into Marlon's face to see if his wife's name made a difference in his expression, only to find him looking right into my eyes. We both gravitated toward each other and before I knew it, our lips met one another's. We were now engaged in a passionate kiss. My arms now wrapped around his neck while his hands were caressing my back.

"Marlon, My God! I am so sorry. I couldn't help myself."

"P, shhh! It wasn't anything I didn't want to happen." Marlon said in a strong voice.

"But what about Stephanie and Derrick?" I said, as tears streamed down my cheeks.

"Well, as for Derrick. Who cares! As for Stephanie. She is not as innocent as you think. I just never bring it up because you already go through so much with Derrick, why add more drama to your plate" Marlon explained.

"I've been having these feelings and felt bad about having them."

"Join the crowd Passion!"

"So, what are you saying?"

"Can I just show you what I'm saying? What will it hurt?" He asked, placing his hands around the back of my neck as he slid a little closer. He began to kiss me slowly up and down my neck, continuing until his kisses made their way down to my chest. We began to undress one another, garment after garment until we were in our birthday suits. I was so impressed with his manhood just by him pressing it against my legs. Marlon seemed to be obsessed with massaging my breast with his tongue, causing my nipples to stand at attention. We kissed and caressed each other until we just could not stand it any longer. "Passion, are you sure you want to do this?"

"Only if you promise it won't hurt our friendship?"

"Trust me! It cannot hurt it. It will only increase the feelings we have been experiencing."

"Well, with that being said, what are you waiting for?" I moaned.

Marlon pushed himself inside me. In that moment I forgot all the drama I was wrapped up in with Derrick and allowed myself to feel passion instead of pain. The frequent strokes made my body explode repeatedly. Before it was all over Marlon made a statement while staring intensely into my eyes.

"Passion, I think I have fallen in love with you."

I didn't respond. Marlon exploded inside of me repeatedly throughout the evening as we continued to explore each other's bodies. Limp from lovemaking, we lay on the sofa, basking in the ambiance of our feelings and each other's embrace.

"Marlon, why did you say what you said a moment ago?"

"Passion, I guess it stemmed from all the talks and being there for one another in our time of need. It just grew on me without me even realizing it."

"I have feelings for you, but I can't say it's love in that way. I hate to admit it, but I still love Derrick's big head ass." We both laughed.

"Well, Passion, I guess we better just keep this between us!"

"Yes. I think we better, but why in the hell am I laying here feeling guilty? I guess it's because since I got married, I've never cheated on Derrick."

"What? Get out of here! For real? Well, I know he has fucked up now then."

"Marlon, I guess you can say that, but enough about Derrick, would you like to shower before going home?"

"Who said I was going home? I told Stephanie that I would probably stay overnight since she got called in for the nightshift."

"Oh," I said, unable to hide my excitement. "So can I encourage you to join me in the shower?"

"Why not!"

That night Marlon and I had sex repeatedly until fatigue was drowning our bodies. I could not sleep in the room Derrick and I shared so, we slept in our guest bedroom instead. We awoke and laid in each other's arms until Marlon prepared to go home. "Passion, is there anything you need me to do before I go?"

"No, I believe we both have done enough for each other!" We found the comment hilarious!

"But on the real Marlon, where do we go from here?"

"Where do you want to go from here? Remember, you love Derrick," he said mockingly, "so let's just take it day by day."

"Ok, good idea! Once again, thanks for being there." We kissed each other on the lips and hugged. It was extremely hard to watch him walk out the door and drive away. He had become my rock and the only person I could trust at this point.

Chapter Twelve

I returned inside the house to prepare myself a cup of coffee, before getting dressed for the day. Moving around in the kitchen my eyes became drawn to the red crystal set that was on display for decoration. It was a family heirloom from my great grandmother and was supposed to be passed down to the eldest daughter of each generation. Coincidentally, I am the youngest daughter, but my mother felt I would take better care of the heirloom than my sister. I recall when this red crystal set was displayed atop of my mother's China Cabinet throughout my childhood. As kids, we knew the value of the set and if we ever broke it, there would be hell to pay. The value of this set made me cherish it more. It is like having something that you know you're not worthy to have, but you have it anyway. I began to wonder why Derrick could not value me the way I value the family heirloom. Instead, he devalued me with all his cheating and secrecy. Looking at the heirloom made me think more of how devalued I was. The color of the red crystal occupied my mind, my heart, and my soul as a meaning of pain, hurt, and sadness. I can imagine that the red of the crystal was not supposed to have this meaning, but at this moment it held it for me. As I kept staring at the decoration. I kept seeing the events of the last day at the hotel. Glimpses of Tay's body lying on the bed and Derrick crawling on the floor kept rolling back and forth in my head. I could not help but wonder how this could have become such a deadly event. How could Derrick be so stupid? No matter how hard I tried to move on from these thoughts and get dressed for the day, I just could not. I even put my shirt on backward from lack of focus. As I sat on the bed struggling to get myself together, I noticed that there was a high number of voicemails on the answering machine. I decided to review them to get my mind off everything else, but the voicemails brought more anguish instead. The first one stated, "This was only the beginning of a deadly battle." The voice was distorted so I could not make out if it were a man or a woman. It was also an unknown caller, therefore there was no number to reference. Now, here I sit wondering what will happen next and who's next on deaths list. Just before I could get up to walk away from the answering machine, the phone rang. Looking at the caller ID I became even more fearful because there was no name on the display, only "caller unknown." Curiosity got the best of me, so I picked up the phone. Nervously, I whispered "hello?" No response, so a bit louder I asked,

"Hello! Can I help you?"

"Passion, its Derrick! I was trying to catch you before you left the house. I called your cell phone and got no answer. Is everything ok?"

"Yes, I'm ok. I was showering and getting dressed. What do you want?"

"Well, the doctor came in this morning and told me everything looks good. The bullet went straight through. He said I can go home today around noon. Can you bring me some clothes from the house?" He asked.

"Ok, I will. Is the doctor sure everything is ok with you or are you rushing him to let you come home?"

"No Passion I am not rushing him, but I am ready to go home."

"Well, give me about an hour and I will be there."

"Ok. You sure you are ok? Your voice sounds a little shaky this morning."

"I'm ok. Just a little disturbed about everything. Well, let me get off here and finish dressing."

"Alright. Passion, I love you."

"Yeah, right Derrick! See you in a little while." Damn! Now I must deal with him at home instead of in the hospital. Some would think that it is sad to say, but I was glad at this point that I did not have to be in his presence all the time. Now that he is being released, I will have to cope with him upfront. Well, no turning back now. I proceeded to gather some clothing for Derrick and headed out the door to pick him up from the hospital. On the way there, I decided to inform Marlon of his release. I should have been notifying Sheryl and Aunt Rose.

"Hello, Passion. What's up? I assume Derrick called you too?"

"Yes, he did. I'm headed up there right now. Are you at the office?"

"Yes, I am, what's wrong? You don't sound right."

"Marlon, I don't want to go pick him up, but I know it's his home too, it's just so different this time."

"Does the way you feel now, have anything to do with what we did last night?"

"No, it doesn't. It's just this time everyone knows about it. In the past, we kept our problems in the house."

"Passion more people knew about the cheating than you think. So, hold your head up. It wasn't your fault. You can't carry the flaws of other individuals."

"I know Marlon, but I still love him. My feelings didn't stop yesterday, but I don't want to remain his wife."

"Ok, I can understand that. That's your decision, but please make sure you're speaking from your heart and not your hurt, so you won't have hurtful regrets."

"Thanks, I will be sure. Well, I've pulled up at the hospital and it looks like he not only called you and me, but he also called Sheryl too. I see her car," I inhaled deeply and sighed, "I'm not sure I'm ready to talk to her today either."

Marlon laughed. "Passion just be yourself as always. Everything is going to work out fine, and if it starts to get stressful today, just think about what a good time we had last night."

"Marlon. You got jokes today I see, but ok. Hopefully, it helps me to overlook the hurt and pain. Well, I will get back to you later, don't work too hard and you be sure to think about it too." I laughed while saying bye.

"Bye P!"

I slowly strolled into the hospital dreading to enter only to physically run into the man I presumed to be Curtis Jones.

"Hello, Ma'am!" He stated.

"Hi. I'm so sorry for bumping into you, I wasn't paying attention. Please excuse me!"

"You're excused." He stated.

It was something about this man that haunted my spirit. He looked at me as though he knew exactly who I was; the same look Candice gave. The funny thing is, I don't know him, but for some reason, I believe I will very soon. I walked around him and proceeded down the hallway to the elevator. Once standing in front of the tall metal doors, I turned to see if the man was gone, only to find him still standing there staring at me. He had an arm brace on his left arm which led me to think of what Derrick said about shooting Curtis Jones. His eyes met mine as we both stared at each other. Just when it seems as though one of us was on the verge of speaking, the elevator doors opened and there stood Sheryl.

"Hey, Passion." She spoke.

"Hello, Sheryl. How are you? I assume Derrick called you too."

"I'm well. No, he didn't. You know today is our normal breakfast date with Aunt Rose, so, I picked her up and decided to come up here for breakfast with him. When I got here, he informed us that he was being released today."

"Oh, ok. I forgot what today is with all that's going on. So, where is Aunt Rose?"

"She is upstairs in the room with him. I went downstairs to visit a coworker who is in the hospital." The doors to the elevator opened and we walked to Derrick's room. Sheryl let me enter the room first. Once inside I noticed that Derrick was up sitting in a chair next to his bed and Aunt Rose was in a chair across the room.

"Good Morning!" I spoke.

"Good Morning, Ma'am!" Aunt Rose said. "You look refreshed."

"Yes, Ma'am. I am a little bit. I'm glad you see how I look and not how I feel."

"Babe, how do you feel?" Derrick asked.

"Derrick, I don't want to discuss it right now. How are you feeling?"

"I'm feeling much better. Especially, now that I'm getting to go home with you." He grinned.

"I wouldn't be so sure of that." I blurted out before I had a chance to think.

"P, what does that mean?" Sheryl asked.

"Forgive me you all. I'm just a little uneasy about this whole situation."

"Well, please don't be treating my brother any type of way. He can go home with me if he needs to. I understand what he has done, but I won't have you mistreating him as payback."

"Sheryl, it's ok. I understand my wife's feelings and she's entitled to them. Please don't come at her like that. We got this!"

I could tell by the look on Sheryl's face that she didn't like Derrick's response, but neither of us said anything after he spoke. I sat down on the other side of his bed glancing over at the TV on the wall, Aunt Rose, however, couldn't let this dead silence remain.

"Sheryl and Passion! We got to remain a family if nothing else. Yes, this is a bad thing that has happened, but also a good thing. It is a wake-up call to us all. We can't take life for granted. Neither can we take each other for granted. We all are in our feelings right now and may say things we don't mean, but what this situation won't do is cause us to be enraged with each other. Do I make myself clear?" Aunt Rose stated.

"Yes ma'am." We mumbled.

"Now, Derrick and Passion! When all this calms down, I think we all need to discuss family issues, but for now, Aunt Rose is going to help keep the peace. Y'all know I can be a mess." She laughed.

"Yes, Ma'am," we all said again in unison. "We will talk as a family later," Derrick wined, "for now can you both just let me, and Passion try to figure things out for ourselves? That's all I'm asking."

"Ok, you got it. I won't say anything to you unless you ask me to." Sheryl said with an attitude.

"Well," said Aunt Rose, "Sheryl let's go downstairs and get breakfast while Derrick gets dressed since that's what we came up here for."

"Ok, Aunt Rose. I think that's a good idea." Sheryl agreed. As they prepared to exit the room, I began to get butterflies in my stomach. I became so nervous once they had left. Not saying a word. Derrick got up and began looking through the bag I brought him. He found what he was looking for and went into the bathroom to start getting dressed. As I sat on the bed watching TV, I wasn't sure if my nervousness was a result of guilt from the previous night's escapade, or was it a result of being alone with a person I now feared? My fear wasn't a fear of intimidation, but a fear of not belonging. This fear made me think about a day Derrick came to visit me in college while I was sitting on the steps having a conversation with a peer.

It was a breezy Wednesday afternoon, Jermaine and I sat on the dorm steps comparing notes for a quiz we had later that day. Once I noticed Derrick's car turning into the parking lot of my dormitory, I became fearful of his reaction. I tried to end the conversation with Jermaine and go inside, but unfortunately, Derrick saw us before we could walk away.

"Passion, what the fuck are you doing?"

"Derrick, what are you talking about? I was just sitting here talking. We were discussing some of the courses that we share, damn! Don't come up here with all that drama!"

"Passion don't play with me girl! Who is that? That's all I'm asking you." Derrick yelled so loudly that Jermaine stopped and turned around.

"Passion, are you ok?" He yelled back.

"Hey, dude! She is ok. Get the fuck on!"

"Jermaine, I'm ok. This is my boyfriend. Just go on, we will talk later."

"No, the fuck you won't be talking to old dude later! Passion you got me fucked up with all that!"

Pushing Derrick in his chest, I yelled at him, "Stop! Let's go to your car before the security guy comes."

"Fuck security! You better start explaining!"

Still going back-and-forth, Derrick and I got into his car and drove off campus. I was fearful if we stayed, he would get himself locked up and me kicked out of school but leaving turned out not to be such a good idea either. The more he drove, the more we yelled at each other, and the angrier Derrick became.

Our argument got so heated that he pulled over at a park and began choking me. This was the first time he resorted to physical harm to make me understand his point of view, but it wouldn't be the last. I believe he wanted to put fear in my heart to keep me from talking to other guys, but even in that moment, his hands around my neck, I was not afraid of the pain he was causing. My fear came from the idea that in his mind, his actions were justified. Now that was truly terrifying. I struggled to free myself from his tightening grip, once he realized I was struggling to breathe he finally set me free. With his release of my neck, there was a release of my emotions. I gasped and coughed as tears flowed like a river's rapid waters. Little did I know my teary-eyed days were just beginning. I stared at him; silent and motionless as he began to take his rage out on the steering wheel. Banging and punching while yelling every obscenity he could think of until he made himself tired. Once is temper tantrum was done, he took me back to campus and left as if nothing had happened.

Chapter Thirteen

"**P**assion, what's wrong?" Derrick stated while pushing my shoulder.

"Huh, what are you talking about?"

"When I came out of the bathroom you were sitting there like a zombie, staring at me with a blank look on your face. Passion, I can tell when something is wrong with you. So, what is it?" I hadn't noticed that Derrick had come out of the bathroom. I inhaled deeply.

"Everything Derrick. I'm not sure if I want to continue in this marriage. I'm so screwed up right now, and I'm afraid of you and I just don't know where our marriage stands at this point. This was the last straw and I just can't go on. I love you, don't get that wrong, but continuing this marriage doesn't' seem possible." Derrick walked over to the other side of the bed and began putting his things in the bag. He acted as though he hadn't heard a word I just said. Once he was all packed, he walked over and sat on the bed next to me.

"I understand what you're saying, but please let's try and work on this one more time. I will go to counseling or whatever you want me to do. Passion, I do love you and I know you have heard this a million times. If we can be honest, we both have done some things, but it's not unrepairable babe. Let's start from this day forward. Can you just please try and see things as I do, P?"

"See things as you see them! Boy, please! If I do that, we surely are through. Derrick, I'm so hurt and frustrated that I can't see past that. All these years I kept saying I was the reason you cheated, but now I see it was you! I can't fulfill you one hundred percent. It's just something inside of you that wants your cake and other's cake too. I love you and I enjoyed being your wife. I tried to please you no matter what, but now, I just think it's time for me to please myself. I need to live life like you, Derrick! Free!"

"Passion, I understand, but what I want is my marriage and you. I do." He began to cry, again. The funny thing is, I couldn't tell if this was sincere or not because Derrick never let anyone see him cry.

"Derrick, I just don't know."

"Please babe! Let's try!"

By this time Aunt Rose and Sheryl walked into the room but they weren't alone. Marlon accompanied them. If anyone were paying me any attention, they would see an awkward expression on my face. Seeing Marlon gave me a jittery feeling inside and I couldn't help these feelings as much as I tried.

"What's up, old boy? Marlon said to Derrick. You look like all is well and you're ready to go."

"Yeah, man. I'm fine. Just a little heartbroken." Derrick turned and looked at me.

"Heart Broken! Is there something we need to know Derrick?" Asked Aunt Rose.

"Well, Aunt Rose my wife is requesting a divorce. I think I fucked up this time! Excuse my language, Auntie this shit hurts worse than getting shot."

"Passion, is that true?" Sheryl asked.

I couldn't respond. I just held my head down and tears began to flow once again. Damn I was tired of crying. The room became extra quiet as though they all wanted to hear my response.

"Passion, you and Derrick need to take time together first. Rethink everything that's happened and how you all can move forward." Aunt Rose replied. "You all got too much at stake to give up. We all make mistakes, but we must learn from them. Don't let this ruin your marriage. Passion, baby you got to fight!" Aunt Rose stated as she began to cry.

"I hear you, but can someone please look at this situation as I do? This isn't the first time he has cheated, shit, this time someone got killed! Not just anyone, she was supposed to be my best friend. Even though she was wrong, I still feel some type of way about her losing her life. Yes, I love my husband, but what can I expect next from him? My Death!?"

"Passion, all Aunt Rose is saying is just to try and work it out. Believe me, sis, I know where you are coming from. You know I've been there. I know y'all love each other. Right now, you are speaking from hurt and pain I believe. Don't make decisions based on your emotions Passion. Let's just get Derrick home and go from there." Sheryl pleaded. The conversations halted and everyone started gathering Derrick's belongings because the nurse was ready to discharge him. After signing the release forms, Derrick was escorted downstairs to the exit. While walking down no one said much at all.

"Mrs. Wilson, can you please bring the car around?"

"Sure, I'll be right back!"

"Passion, I'll walk with you to get the car," Marlon advised.

"Marlon, I asked Derrick for a divorce. I thought about everything as I drove here this morning. I believe I'm going to move back home for a while until I can see things a little clearer. I just need to get away."

"Can I come?" Marlon asked, as he laughed. "But on a serious note, Passion, did I make it more complicated for you last night?"

"No. I wanted it just like you did. Matter of fact, I can't stop thinking about it. Wow, we better stop this talk right now because I'm feeling the right feelings at the wrong time."

"Well, I'll let you drive on around to pick your husband up." Marlon continued to be playful.

"Are you following us home?"

"Yes. I'm coming over in about thirty minutes. I got a stop to make first. Or should I wait a little longer?"

"No, 30 minutes is long enough, I don't want to be alone with him."

"Ok, I'll see you later." Marlon leaned over and kissed me on my forehead. His kiss felt so comforting causing me to get a tingling feeling in the seat of my pants. As he walked away, I noticed myself watching him. "Snapback Passion and drive up there," I said to myself as I proceeded slowly to the exit. Derrick got in and we drove away in dead silence. That ride seemed to be the longest most silent ride I had experienced in a very long time. As we turned onto our street, my anxiety began to creep in.

"I'm so glad to see this house again," Derrick said.

"I can imagine you are glad," I said, in a sarcastic voice.

"Passion, I don't think you can. Right now, I just want to thank God. He allowed me to feel better today and live through yesterday. Ever since this happened, I wanted to just run away and fold up. I didn't want to face you or anyone else for that matter, but I can't run from what I created. All I can do is take things one day at a time and face my consequences."

"So, if you're so ready to face your consequences. Why not agree to a divorce?"

"Passion, you back on that again!"

"Yes! I will be on it until you agree to give it to me." Opening the door from inside the garage, I walked on into the house. I didn't even grab any of his bags. Better yet, I didn't even make sure he got into the house. I headed straight to the bedroom to make sure everything was ok and there was no evidence of what happened last night. Derrick entered the bedroom and placed his bags in the corner. I had gone inside the closet to remove my shoes and put on my slippers. Upon coming out of the closet Derrick met me at the foot of the bed. He placed his arms around my waist and stared into my face. He was trying to kiss my lips, but unfortunately for him, his lips met the back of my hands as I blocked his kiss.

"Passion, for real! Not even one kiss?"

"Derrick, you just don't get it. This is not just a slap on your wrist again. This shit hurts so bad that I can't even stand to look at you."

Derrick took his arms from around me and backed up as if he were saying go on. I walked around him and strolled up the hallway to our den. I flung myself on the couch, turned on the TV and started searching for something to detour my mind from being here with him. Then the sound of the doorbell rang out twice. "Huh, who could this be? I sure hope it's Marlon," I mumbled under my breath as I got back up. "Who is it?" As I looked out the peephole of the front door.

"Passion, it's us!" Yelled Sheryl. It was Sheryl and Aunt Rose. They had decided to come over to make sure Derrick got in ok. I opened the door and walked back to the den.

"That was rude Passion. You opened the door rudely." Sheryl said.

"Sheryl, this is just like your home. Plus, we just saw one another." I laughed.

"Ok, I thought I was going to have to put these hands on you!" Aunt Rose said jokingly.

Derrick was coming up the hallway.

"Why y'all didn't shut the door Auntie?" He asked.

"Because Marlon is parking," Sheryl said.

"Oh, Ok!"

Everyone made their way into the den. Marlon came in and shut the door, he had no choice but to sit on the other end of the sofa on which I had stretched my legs out. Derrick was reclining in his favorite chair and Sheryl and Aunt Rose sat on the love seat.

"So, Derrick have you heard anything else from the investigation?" Sheryl asked.

"No! I guess they are still looking into everything before they contact me again."

"Well, I spoke with some of my friends in the department who are handling the case. They got some strong leads and a lot of witnesses who saw the guy running from the room. They have a good description of what he was wearing as well." Sheryl stated.

"Sheryl, I'm not worried about it, in due time he will get his," Derrick said.

"What's that's supposed to mean? You better sit your ass down somewhere and let the police handle this." Sheryl said angrily.

"Yeah, Ok!" He smirked.

"I think on that note we need to pray," Aunt Rose insisted. "I've just about had enough of the old devil trying to destroy my family!" Those who know Aunt Rose knows she can be a mess and a blessing. She is the Aunt who will tell you like it is, but at the same time put the word of God on you.

"Do you all think I'm playing? I want us to stand up and pray right now!" Aunt Rose demanded.

We gradually removed ourselves from our seats and met in the middle of the den. We grabbed hands and lowered our heads. The funny thing for me was Derrick on the left side and Marlon on my right side. What an awkward moment. There I stood holding the hands of the two men that held pieces of my heart. I needed a lot of prayer just like the men who were holding each of my hands. As Aunt Rose began to pray, I could feel the trembling of Derrick's hand while it embraced mine.

"Father God, we come before you today to ask for your protection over our family. Let no other harm fall on us. Keep them away from accidents such as yesterday. Allow no evil to influence their hearts and mind. Cover them with the precious Blood of Christ. Take charge over them so that they do not strike their foot against the stones being thrown at them. We may not be with one another all the time daily, but I trust that you, Lord, are always with us. Keep them safe today and all other days. Please allow them to always give glory to you. Give them peace of mind so that they may not worry about anything. Guard their hearts and minds so that they may only display love instead of hate, anger, or bitterness. Amen."

Chapter Fourteen

As Aunt Rose closed the prayer with Amen and we all joined in to say the same, I returned to lay back down on the sofa. Aunt Rose and Sheryl returned to the love seat, but Derrick and Marlon exited the den and went outside in the backyard.

"I wonder what that talk is going to be about!" Said Sheryl.

"I can only imagine," Aunt Rose said. "Passion, are you ok, and have you thought about what I told you and Derrick at the hospital?" Aunt Rose asked.

"Yes, Ma'am! I'm dealing with it in my own way. I trust God will bring me out of it ok as well. As far as the divorce, it's still a great thought in my head."

"Passion, let Auntie share some things with you if that's ok?"

"Yes, Ma'am! Go for it."

"Babe, are you familiar with the word cliché?"

"Yes, Ma'am," I said.

"Well, I had a friend who told me to think about the old saying of what goes around comes back around like a cliché. For the life of me, I didn't see it as one at first. I had to look up the definition of a cliché. The word cliché is defined as a phrase or opinion that is overused and betrays a lack of original thought. See, we have used this phrase so much as a warning to others to let them know they may have gotten away with something, but it may come back around to them.

"Passion, I said that to say this babe. What happened is simply a cliché for Derrick and your friend. They had gotten away with their love affair for however long and in return it blew up in their faces. Don't get Auntie wrong, no one deserves to die for cheating, but we all need to think about other's frame of minds. Some people can't handle betrayal. I'm sorry for her family and I'm even sorrier for you Passion, but I need you and Derrick to really look at yourselves in general. Passion, you even stated Derrick has done this repeatedly and you've stayed. Babe, you've stayed for a reason. Focus on that reason and see if it's worth moving forward with him. I'm not just saying this because Derrick is my nephew, but because I love the both of you. Let his karma be that he must look you in the face daily knowing what he's done. To me that's the best revenge you can give a person. Wayne Dyer said it best. How people treat you is their karma; how you react is yours! So, Passion if a divorce is what you truly want, then get it, if you want to be his karma and stay married, then so be it. Just know Aunt Rose loves you regardless and will always be here for you. I'm through preaching now!" Aunt Rose said, with tears filling her eyes.

I totally understood every word she was saying, but at this point the words were just that. Words. I didn't say anything after Aunt Rose finished talking. I just nodded my head to let her know I heard her and understood. I was kind of hoping the subject would change since I didn't respond with words. But, unfortunately, Sheryl took this as an opportunity to ask further questions.

"Passion, so you say you got a call that said catch them if you could. Is that right?"

"Yes, Sheryl."

"So, on the call an address was giving too?"

"Yes, Sheryl."

"Passion, I know I'm frustrating you, but I'm just trying to make all this make since. I just don't want anything else to come out because then won't be able to help either of you at all." She explained.

Derrick and Marlon walked through the door, "perfect timing," I grinned. They walked through the kitchen and out the garage door, talking as they walked through, but I couldn't make out what they were saying. We all looked at each other and shrugged as the men exited the house. To escape Sheryl's interrogation, I excused myself to the restroom. I locked the door and sat on the chair in front of my vanity. As I sat there passing time, I glanced over at the shower and smiled as I began to daydream of the day before. The thoughts of Marlon and I caressing one another and moaning as we explored each other's bodies was all I could think of. I closed my eyes and wished that moment were happening all over again. I rubbed different parts of my body fantasizing as though they were Marlon's hands instead of my own. I tilted my head back and bit my bottom lip as I remembered the softness of his lips on my body. A light moan managed to escape my lips. Just as I was preparing to whisper his name, "Mar...," "Knock Knock!" I heard at the door, nearly causing me to have a heart attack!

"Passion!" Aunt Rose called out.

"Yes, Ma'am!" My voice cracked.

"We are getting ready to go and we wanted to let you know. Call us if you need anything and remember what I said babe, Ok?"

"Ok, Auntie. I sure will. Love you and thank you so much!" I stated.

"Love you too! Have a good rest of the day!"

I waited a while before I came out of the bathroom. I wanted to make sure that they had left before I went back into the den. Derrick and Marlon had also returned, only this time Derrick was sitting where Marlon sat previously. I guess Derrick wanted to be near me, oh well for his bad judgement. I decided to sit in the recliner, giving him a smirk to let him know I peeped his game. Marlon and Derick both busted out in laughter, I guess Derrick had planned this little stunt.

"What is funny?" I asked.

Derrick responded, "Passion, you are something else! Why wouldn't you sit on the sofa this time? You really don't want to be close to me that bad?"

"And you are absolutely correct." I said, clapping my hands. "Oh, ok. My bad."

"Well, since you guys seem to be okay, I'm going to head out too. Derrick, if you need something let me know, same for you Passion, I'm just a call away."

"Ok, Marlon! Thanks, man again for everything." Derrick stated.

They did their man hang shack to say goodbye, Marlon kissed me on my forehead as usual and I smiled to myself knowing that Derrick had no clue that the kiss meant more now than it ever did before. I walked Marlon to the door so I could set the alarm, plus, I wanted to get one last glimpse of him before he left. I must admit that my feelings are a little deeper than I would like for them to be, but Marlon must never know that. I opened the door and Marlon proceeds to walk away, but quickly turns back to gently caress my cheek. I puckered my lips offering an air kiss to reciprocate his subtle display of affection. I sighed as I slowly closed the door and headed back into the den. Derrick had laid down on the sofa and started to watch a movie.

"What movie is this Derrick?"

"I don't know the title of it, but it looks pretty good so far. If I had to guess, it may be a cartel movie."

"Oh, ok."

Without saying another word. I made my way to the sofa and stood over him. He looked up as though he didn't know what to expect.

"Can I please lay beside you?" I asked.

"Sure, I've been waiting on this all day!" He stated excitingly.

He scooted back on the sofa and I laid next to him. We usually did this when we watched movies in the den. I had always felt a sense of comfort and security when he wrapped his arms around me. As much as I hated to admit it, it's kind of a good feeling, even though I was still mad at him, this moment, was good. We lay wrapped in each other's arms unsure of what the other was thinking, but enjoying the gesture of love, as though the past nearly 48 hours had not happened. My body was relaxed, but my mind was still tense. I just needed to be reassured that he meant what he said earlier about his love for me. Did he still love me or am I simply the one who won't go away; the last one standing? I guess for now. I am. The more the movie went on the more similarities of yesterday it resembled. The movie even had a scene in which a man was shot at a hotel. The only difference was there was no woman in the shootout.

Watching this movie brought my questions from the back of my mind to the edge of my lips.

"Derrick."

"Yes, Babe. What's up?"

"Can you be truthful with me?"

"I'll try."

"Why Tay?"

"Because she was easy!"

"Really Derrick! Easy is what you like?"

"Passion, you said truth. You can't see past the fact that I am your husband, and she was your 'bestie.'" Like you said earlier, I've cheated repeatedly, and you stayed, but this time it's different because she was your friend. Babe understand what I mean when I say easy. I didn't have to work hard to have her. If you look back, she always wanted what you had. You just always try and give others the benefit of the doubt. I'm not trying to sound arrogant Passion, but all my life women have just made things easy for me. I crawl inside their heads and trick them into giving me the secrets of their hearts. I drown them in manipulation and then give them the illusions of their dreams. I guess I can say I mastered the game of deception."

"So, you are saying in so many words that I was easy too?"

"You started out as a challenge and that's why I fell for you, I just had to have you all to myself. Then as I learned you, I guess you can say that, yes, you became easy too. The difference though was that you had so many other qualities that I loved, I refused to let you go. The others were basic, they never meant anything to me. They were just entertainment."

"So, Candice is easy too? You've been messing with her for a very long time."

"Yes, Candice is easy but if I be truthful, she was the first woman I fell in love with and the last to break my heart, so for her, it's payback."

"I don't understand that. Payback?"

"Yes, because she wants me as her husband but because of what she did with Curtis Jones, I only play with her mind. She could never fill your shoes."

"Oh, so I get it now, Curtis steps in and took her from you, so, you mess around with her to get back at him."

"Something like that. He and I were best friends, and he went behind my back and slept with her. He bought her things, spoiled her, because he knew that at that time, I couldn't afford to do it. Oh, but when I started to shine brighter than he was, she wanted back on the team. It was too little too late; I was too far gone from the feelings I once had for her." He said, shaking his head.

"I totally understand now. So, for all these years. You basically been playing the get back game. Just when I want to believe your love is sincere for me. I find out more devastating shit!" I snapped!

"Passion, you said be truthful. You are missing the whole point. Yes, I've played the get back game with Candice, but babe I Love You! Can't you see that's why I never leave you, Damn! I guess I have an issue with being faithful to one woman, but can we talk about this another time?" He yelled.

"Fine!" I huffed, "I think I got a little more information than I was searching for anyway."

I stormed out the den and went to the bedroom. I slung my body across the bed and the flood gates opened. I wept so loudly that I barely recognized my own voice. Usually, when I am upset Derrick comes to console me, but even he could tell this sob was different, he remained in the den as I struggled to comprehend what I just heard.

Chapter Fifteen

As I laid in bed, I couldn't help but ask God; what should I do next? Why is all this happening to me? Should I stay or should I go? Now, in my heart and mind, I know I'm no better than Derrick. Just last night I slept with his best friend. I let my feelings cloud my better judgement and the sad part is it wasn't even revenge on Derrick and Tay. It was truly because my feelings for Marlon are genuine. Either way am I destined to experience the cliché Aunt Rose talked about? Is my karma going to come back around to me for acting on my feelings? It sounded good when she was saying these things about Derrick, but now as I apply it to myself, it doesn't feel good at all. What does feel good is the way Derrick talked about women being easy, not knowing that Marlon took his place for just one night. Wonder if he felt the same about men, and if he ever considered how women too can manipulate to get what they want. I honestly could care less, all that keeps going through my mind is who made love to me the best? I bet if you asked Derrick, he would swear he will always be the best because he was my first. As I lay there staring at the ceiling, it became a mirror, showing reflections of the first time Derrick and I made love. I'm somewhat ashamed now of the place in which I lost my virginity, but at the time I was elated. Whoever says making love in a car isn't okay for your first time, must didn't do it right! Derrick picked me up from school and we were cruising down Neal Street talking about how much we were feeling each other. Suddenly, Derrick decided that stopping in the park on a cold November night would be a good idea.

"Derrick, why are we stopping here?" I asked.

"Passion, I just want to talk underneath the stars."

"It's cold out tonight and I think we can see the stars while driving." I laughed.

"P come on. I'm trying to be romantic. You're always asking for romance, but now you've spoiled the moment. How is school going?"

"School is fine and before you ask, no, no one has been flirting with me! Everyone is under the impression that I date this big-time drug dealer, so they are scared to even speak to me."

"Oh, yeah! Is that right?" He chuckled.

"Shiddd, that is good. That mean my goods will remain in tack and untouched."

"What's that's supposed to mean?"

"Passion, Ok! Enough is enough. Just let me show you why I need you untouched."

"Derrick, show me how?"

"Like this." Derrick began to kiss me. Then he started to rub my breast working his way down my body.

"Derrick, stop! I'm not quite ready for all of that yet!"

"Come on Passion! You know I've waited long enough, plus. I love you!"

"You love me! For real?"

"Yes, I love you!"

"I Love you too!"

"Then Passion, why keep me waiting?"

I knew I shouldn't have kept going, but I couldn't stop now. I was feeling things in parts of my body that I had never experienced before. My nipples were hard as bricks, I had a tingling sensation between my legs, and the more Derrick kissed me, the sensations grew more and more intense. He continued to kiss and caress every inch of my body, slowly beginning to undress me.

"Derrick, babe not here in the car! I didn't want my first time to be in a car! I kind of wanted it to be a little more romantic."
"It is special because we are together under the stars, besides Passion there is no one out here!"

Before I had a chance to refute, he was already inserting himself inside me.

"Ohhhh, Derrick that hurts! Please be gentle and go slowly!" I whispered.

"Ok, babe, just relax and the pain will ease up." He moaned. After a minute or two, he was right, the pain began to fade, and pleasure began to enter. My body exploded repeatedly as

Derrick continued each stroke in and out of me. When we both had reached our peak. Derrick climbed back in the driver seat and advised me to get used to this, because there is no turning back now.

"Derrick, what does that mean?"

"You're all mine now. I'm your first and I'm going to make sure I'm your last!" He said strongly.

"Uhh! My first and my last!" As I snapped back from daydreaming. I bet he thought he would be my last. Looks like Marlon will be after all the shit that occurred this week. I was so wrapped up in my memories, I didn't notice Derrick entering our bedroom.

"Passion, were you talking to someone?"

"No, Derrick, just thinking out loud."

"Can I come in here with you?" He asked.

"It's your home isn't it?"

"Also, can we talk now?"

"About what?"

"Us."

"Derrick, there is no use. You made that clear the day you made the choice to be in the hotel."

"Ok, P! Shit, I've tried repeatedly. I'm tired off asking. If you want a divorce, then you can fucking have one! I'm not going to keep kissing your ass." He said angrily.

"Well, well! I didn't ask you too!"

"You want me to act an ass. I will. You can stay your ass in this room, and I will go into the guess room until things get straightened out. You just remember this is what you wanted!" He yelled.

"Boy gone on somewhere."

Derrick went out the room and back into the den. I continued to lay on the bed. I had finally got him to agree to a divorce but was that really what I wanted. Or was I just holding the idea over his head, because of what he had done to me?

Chapter Sixteen

After all that has happened this week, I felt like life was ending for me. Derrick had repeatedly apologized, but that wasn't enough for me. My heart had been shattered and battered. How could he possibly think I would let this blow over that easy? I guess he felt this way because of all the times I forgave his cheating games in the past. Another nightfall came and we were still in different areas of the house. I decided it was best for me to refrain from communicating with him right now because I know his temper, and only he knows the thoughts in his mind. I didn't want to send him over the edge since I already knew he was upset about the divorce. After a nice hot shower, I climbed into bed. While struggling to fall asleep, all I could visualize was the scene from the Shamrock Hotel room and wonder what really happened that morning. It had been a week, and the investigation was still open and there had been no significant changes in the case. I could hear my mother's voice in the back of my mind," Baby, listen to your inner voice when it speaks to you, it will never steer you wrong." I laid there looking at the ceiling, wishing my mother were here now. Only if I had taken heed to her warnings.

"Baby, that young man is going to bring you a lot of heart ache." She would proclaim.

"I know how it is when you think you're in love, and nobody can tell you otherwise." As I reflect on her words, I remember how beautiful her angelic face was as she lie in complete peace. My mother, my friend, my comforter had left me. My mother was my best friend. We had a relationship like no other, and I will never forget the day my life changed forever. On January 18, 2000 at 11:20pm, my phone rang.

"Passion, a trembling voice cried out, this is Aunt Shirlene. You need to come home ASAP! Martha had a stroke this morning and is in the hospital."

"Ok, Auntie. I'm on my way! Let me tell Derrick so he can bring me home."

"Ok, drive careful and see you in a few."

"Derrick get up! We have got to go to Garden City. My mom had a stroke."

"What?" Derrick Said as he turned away from me.

"Derrick, please get up! I can't drive right now. I'm too nervous babe!"

"Ok, Ok, babe. I hear you." He said, as he sat up in the bed. We got dressed and rushed from Tenison to head for my hometown. Once we entered the city, I could tell everything was still the same. The houses were still in the same shape, and everyone seemed to be doing the same things, either hanging out at the car wash or just riding around in their cars. We arrived at the hospital, only to find that I was already too late. My mother had died an hour ago. My family had decided just to wait until I got there to tell me, instead of calling me on the road. I entered the emergency room but couldn't find my family. I asked the front desk attendant if she could tell me which room Martha Benson was in. She looked up at me and advised that she was on the first floor in ICU. As Derrick and I walked through the crowd of my family members standing in the hall. I knew something was wrong. My brothers were all crying and my uncle who was very close to my mom couldn't look me in my face. Aunt Shirlene was always the strong hold of our family.

"Passion!" Derrick yelled.

"What Derrick!" I replied.

"Babe, your mother is gone!" He answered.

"Oh, my GOD!" I screamed. I fell on the floor yelling and screaming. "Oh, No!"

Everyone rushed over to me. They placed me in a chair.

"I want to see her!"

"Come on babe, the doctor said we can go back there!" Aunt Shirlene explained.

I walked down a long hall and finally arrived at the door I dreaded to walk through. Pushing the door open and seeing my mother seemed so drastic. Walking over and staring at her made tears flood my face. She looked so peaceful and beautiful, like an angel sleeping. They say when most people have strokes, their faces are disfigured, but my mother looked as though she had finally gotten the rest, she needed so badly. It was at this point, my tears stopped, and I knew she had gone home to be with the Lord. I kissed her and apologized for not being there at her last hour. For some reason, my heart believed she heard me. With Derrick beside me and my aunt across from me, I turned and walked out the room. Somehow, I knew things would never be the same for me. A link of my heart had just been broken apart.

Knock! Knock!

"What!" I yelled as I rolled over in the bed. The knock on the door had stopped me from dreaming of my mom.

"Can I come in?"

"Derrick, what do you want?" I asked, as I noticed my face was wet from crying.

"I want to ask you something."

"About what?"

The door opened and Derrick came in. He sat on the other side of the bed.

"Passion, tomorrow can you take me to the doctor's office? He left a message saying he needs for me to come into the office. He needs to talk to me about my results and recovery process. I understand you don't want to do anything for me right now, but can you just please drive me there?"

I rolled over and looked at him only to say yes when I knew I wanted to say, "you got to be a damn fool to ask me something like that!" For some reason I knew it was more to it than that, I felt like he wanted me to be by his side even though he knew he didn't deserve it.

"Ok! You asked. Now get out!"

"Girl, you still pushing it. But I'll do that P!"

Derrick left the room and I rolled back over to go back to sleep. I awoke that morning to the sound of music playing. I opened the door and saw Derrick struggling to put on his pants, still sore from the wounds of his infidelity.

"Derrick, would you like me to help you?" I asked, with frustration.

"If you don't mind! I would really appreciate it."

I walked in the room and pulled his pants up. While I was attempting to help with his shirt Derrick grabbed me.

"Passion, I really love you! Can we please try and work this out?"

Not saying a word, I helped him put his shoes on, and walked away. Now that he was ready, I could focus on myself. I began searching my closet for my outfit of the day. I had decided that from now on I would look my best to remind my husband what he used to own. I pulled out the tightest pair of jeans I owned and a low-cut fitting blouse with ruffles around the collar. For some reason, Derrick always liked me in boots, so it was only right that I put on the pair he loved to see me walk in. As I exited our bedroom, I could feel Derrick's eyes scanning over my body.

"Passion, you sure look nice!"

"Are you ready to go? There are some things that I need to do today as well."

"Yes, Ma'am." He said jokingly.

Once again, the ride seemed so long due to the dead silence in the car. Neither of us said a single word. Once we arrived at the doctor's office, our silence continued as we graciously waited for the doctor in the surprisingly empty waiting room. "Mr. Wilson, the doctor will see you now!" stated the nurse.

Derrick and I proceeded down a long hall, before entering an office composed of two chairs opposite the desk in which a white male sat with his hands clasped together in front of him. I had expected to see the doctor who had taken care of Derrick while he was in ICU, however, this was a different doctor. I must admit this doctor was very attractive with black hair, well groomed, and his uniform well pressed.

"Have a seat Mr. and Mrs. Wilson."

"How are you guys doing today?" He asked.

"Just fine!" Derrick responded.

I guess the doctor could feel the tension between us, especially since I still hadn't uttered a single word.

"Well, the reason I asked you to come in today and bring your wife is because there are some very important factors that could hinder a speedy recovery."

"If you don't mind me asking, what are you talking about sir? You're not the same doctor from the ICU. I stated loudly."

"No, Ma'am. I'm not, but I did have a chance to meet your husband prior to him being discharged. Dr. Henderson referred him to me to assist with his recovery."

"Ok, I'm sorry. This is just so much for me right now. Please continue."

Derrick looked as though he already knew why we were here, and I was embarrassing him.

"Well, after receiving your test results Mr. Wilson, your blood work came back with some concerns. It seems that your charts are showing some abnormalities. Now, before we confirm anything for sure, I would like to do further testing, however, the results we received show that you are positive for HIV."

"Come again doctor!" Derrick screamed. "I know that's a damn lie! You must've gotten my charts mixed up with someone else!"

"Mr. Wilson, I wish that were the case, but unfortunately it's not. Mrs. Wilson, we will need to test you as well."

"Ma'am?" the doctor asked.

I couldn't say a word, I couldn't move, I couldn't blink. I felt like I couldn't breathe. Tears rolled down my face as I sat staring at Derrick, I really wanted to shoot him now.

"I heard you doctor." I stated, not taking my eyes off the side of Derrick's face. I couldn't help myself, before I knew it, I slapped Derrick so hard the sound echoed throughout the hallway.

"Mrs. Wilson, stop please! There is no violence in this office!" The doctor yelled.

"Sir, I'm sorry for the disrespect, but this is just too much! Derrick, I always knew you would bring something home! But never this. I thought maybe a baby or some other type of disease. But HIV?! You Bitch, I hate you!" I cried.

My mind played back so many instances in which I could hear myself saying to Derrick, "While you're out there whoring, you better not bring me nothing home!" This time it's really happening, not just me saying it, it's my reality, I'm living it. I just sat in the chair staring back at the doctor.

"So, what do I need to do to get tested? I might as well get this over with!" I asked.

"Well, we will need to get some blood from you both today and within twenty-four hours I will have the results."

"Doctor, is there a chance that I could be negative, and Derrick's test are incorrect?" I asked.

"Yes, Mrs. Wilson. There could be a strong chance. Now, I must ask the both of you. How many other sexual partners have you encountered within the last ten years?"

"Huh! It will take days for my husband to compile that list!" Even with all my sarcasm. Derrick still hadn't replied.

"Mr. Wilson. Are you ok?" the doctor asked.

"Yes! I'm just trying to grasp all of this. Let's just take the other tests."

"Ok, you guys follow me."

We were placed in two separate rooms to complete the testing. While waiting on the nurse, I couldn't help but cry out, "Lord, please! This cannot be happening. I don't think I can take anything else."

"Ma'am are you ok?" The nurse asked.

"Please, just give me a moment!"

"Ok. Let me know if I can be of any help Mrs. Wilson!"

I hadn't realized that I was on the floor, with the nurse's assistance, I sat back on the exam table. The nurse gave me a moment to get myself together before proceeding with the blood samples. Ma'am, the doctor will contact you within twenty-four hours with your results. Is there anything else I can assist you with at this time?"

"No, thank you!"

I walked out the doctor's office like a zombie. Everything was blank for me the rest of the evening. I don't even remember the drive home. All I remember is a broken record playing in my head; "positive for HIV."

"Passion! Get out of the car and come on in the house." Derrick said.

"What, why in the hell are you even talking to me! Do you know what you have done! All because you can't keep your dick in your pants, I may have a disease that could someday kill me! Is that all you have to say? Come in the house? I should have shot you and Tay my damn self! Or maybe, I should just shoot you now!" I cried, "But what good would that do now! Still won't' help me! Get away from me Derrick, Please!"

I ran into the house, straight to the bedroom, and slammed the door.

"Passion, let's talk for real!" Derrick screamed from behind the door. "It's too late to turn back. I need to be honest with you and you need to be honest with me. Yes, I fucked up our lives, but all we can do is pray and hope for the best. Whether you believe me or not, I really hope you're not positive. Hell, I pray I'm not either, but you are right, you don't deserve this. I can't change the past and I'm so sorry for ever entering your life. I'll give you a divorce Passion. So, you can get on with your life without me."

I didn't really hear everything he said, so I opened the door to see him walking toward the den; I followed him. Moments later the doorbell was ringing, it was Marlon. By the look on his face, he wasn't too happy about something himself. He pushed past me and followed Derrick into the den. I followed behind both.

"Can I come in with you all too?" I asked.

"I don't' have a problem with that, Derrick, do you?" Marlon asked.

"No, Passion. You already know what Marlon and I are about to discuss." He said.

We all sat down in different areas of the den. I was so nervous, because if Derrick were about to tell Marlon what we learned at the doctor office, all hell would break loose.

"Derrick, what did you want to tell me? You said you needed to tell me this in person and you need me more now than anything." Marlon asked.

"Marlon!" Derrick said hesitantly. "We just left the doctor's office, and he blew us the fuck away with what he said."

"What he say, man?"

"Shit! He explained to me and Passion that my blood work came back positive for HIV! He had Passion to take a test and gave me a retest to be sure."

Marlon was silent as he looked at Derrick. Then he looked over at me. I was already looking at him because I wanted to see the reaction on his face. He shook his head repeatedly while biting on the side of his lip. Then he looked back at Derrick and softly spoke.

"So, are you for real?" Marlon asked.

"Yes, man. We retested and should hear something in twenty-four hours to be sure."

"So, what are you all going to do?"

"Man, we can't do anything but live life and do whatever the doctor tells us." Derrick stated. "Crazy thing is they want everyone we have had sex with in the last ten years. I don't even know where some of those females are this shit is so fucked up!"

"Passion, you ok?" Marlon asked.

I couldn't say yes or no. I just stared at him with eyes full of tears. Marlon came over and sat next to me. He put his arms around my shoulder. This made me cry harder. Most would have thought this would cause suspicion and Derrick to question Marlon's actions, but since Marlon has always been our voice of reason, this didn't faze Derrick at all. Besides, Derrick was so ashamed that he left the room, and moments later, I heard the garage door open.

Chapter Seventeen

For I was hungry, and you gave me something to eat, I was thirsty, and you gave me something to drink, I was a stranger and you invited me in, I needed clothes and you clothed me, I was sick, and you looked after me, I was in prison and you came to visit me. Then the righteous will answer him, Lord, when did we see you hungry and feed you, or thirsty and give you something to drink? When did we see you a stranger and invite you in, or needing clothes and clothe you? When did we see you sick or in prison and go to visit you? The King will reply, truly I tell you, whatever you did for one of the least of these brothers and sisters of mine, you did for me." Marlon recited this to me as we sat on the couch. He went on to say, "Passion, this should be an eye opener for us all. I'm in awe right now! All I could think about was the scripture of Matthew twenty-five, verses thirty-five through forty as Derrick told me the news. Now we are all worried about having something because we have destroyed each other's trust, loyalty, and bodies. How can we honestly say we are friends when no one cares about the other's feelings? I guess this is God's way of showing us." Marlon said.

"Funny you should say that Marlon. I guess we can ask ourselves now was it really work us acting on the feelings we shared the other night."

"Passion, we sure are about to find out when these test results come back."

"So, are you going to tell Stephanie?"

"Only when your test results come back!"

We heard the door open back up, so we paused our conversation. Derrick walked back in and said, "Passion, did Marlon comfort you like you needed just then?"

"Derrick, why do you ask that?" I said, defensively.

"Because I know you find comfort in his words. That's why I left, so you could vent to him openly and feel a little better."

"Well, you were right! Now sit down we all need to talk. Derrick, I am not sure how we are going to move forward, but please be honest with me! Do you know where you could have contracted this from?"

"Passion, I don't have a clue! Can we just wait until the results come back to discuss this further?"

"Derrick, you always want to talk later! I just need answers. Can you please stop making me look like the villain?"

"Passion, no one is making you look like anything! I'm just tired right now and really need a break from all this shit!" Derrick yelled.

"Ok, you need a break. I will give you a big break!"

I got up and left the room. I can only imagine what the conversation was when I left.

"Marlon, she is really freaking the fuck out!" Derrick said. "It's worse than the time when she lost the baby."

"Damn! I forgot all about that D." Marlon said.

Three years after Derrick and I got together. I had a miscarriage. I had started working at the law firm with Stephanie after graduating from college. I had received my paralegal degree and I was ready to put it to use. Stephanie got me hired on at the law firm of Watson and Watson. She had been employed there for two years and was able to pull some strings to get me on. It was a hot summer day and I had just returned from lunch. As I was entering the building with Derrick, I dropped my keys in front of the door. As I bent over to retrieve them, I felt a sharp pain in my side and stomach. It was a pain I had never experienced before, but it soon faded after I am standing back up. I proceeded into the office and took a seat at my desk. Stephanie came in and began chatting about lunch when the pains appeared again.

"Wow!" I yelled.

"What's wrong Passion?" Stephanie asked.

"I'm not quite sure. I keep having sharp pains in my side and stomach."

Stephanie gave me a long look with raised eyebrows, "Pain in your stomach? Could you be pregnant?"

"Pregnant! Come on Stephanie! Girl no." I responded laughing, but as I thought about it, I really couldn't say yes, or no. Derrick and I were having unprotected sex, but I had not experienced any other symptoms.

"Well, Passion. I'm going to get back to work, but if you need me, I'm right down the hall."

Just as Stephanie turned to walk away. I yelled, "Stephanie wait!" I screamed, "Something is wrong. I'm having really bad pain in my stomach and I can feel it in my chest and back." I need to get to the hospital now" I cried.

"Ok, Passion! Let me tell Mr. Watson that we need to leave ASAP!" Stephanie left frantically and quickly returned with her keys and purse. She and another coworker helped me into the car as my body convulsed with pain. Once inside, I made a quick call to Derrick to let him know what was going on.

"Hello!" Derrick said.

"Derrick, I'm headed to the hospital!" I said tearfully.

"Why? What's wrong?" He asked.

"I'm not sure! I started having unbearable pain in my stomach and it's hard for me to sit up straight."

"Are you driving there?"

"No, Stephanie is driving me."

"Ok, I will meet y'all there! Stop crying P! It's going to be ok. I love you babe!"

I hung up the phone, holding my stomach as Stephanie drove fiercely to the hospital. I couldn't help but let out a loud cry due to the pain I was experiencing. Finally, we arrived and went into the emergency room. Due to my pain level and the height of my blood pressure, I was admitted and put into a room immediately. The ER nurse began hooking me up to the necessary equipment, then she asked me the ultimate question: "Ma'am, is there any way you may be pregnant?"

"There is a possibility, but I don't think I am!" Stephanie shook her head.

"Ok. We will need for you to take a pregnancy test just to be sure. I understand you are in pain, but I will need you to provide a sample of urine before I can give you anything for it."

She assisted me to the restroom, and I provided her with what she needed. As soon as I got back on the bed, the door opened and in came Derrick and Marlon.

"Babe, are you ok?" Derrick asked as he walked over and kissed me on the lips.

"Yes, but still in a lot of pain." I moaned.

"Stephanie, thanks for driving her here."

"No problem Derrick. We are family!"

Derrick sat on the side of the bed holding my hand. As time passed, we all sat there talking and watching TV until the doctor finally entered the room. He spoke to everyone and walked over to the other side of the bed.

"Hello, Mrs. Wilson! I see you're not feeling well today?"

"No, Sir. Not at all."

"Well, I think I can give you a little relief. The pregnancy test came back positive, unfortunately, I believe you are experiencing symptoms of a miscarriage. There were traces of blood in your urine and from the looks of these monitors, other things are happening as well. So, I would like to do a sonogram of your stomach and chest just to be sure."

"Are you serious?" Derrick asked. I didn't say anything, just laid there as tears accumulated in my eyes.

"Yes, Sir. Would you be the father?"

"Yes, Sir! I'm her husband."

Shortly after the doctor left the nurses began several tests. While in the middle of the sonogram, I started to bleed very heavily. The nurse notified the doctor, and they took the proper measures to assist me during the miscarriage. After it was all said and done, I became angry and annoyed about any and everything. This would have been my first child and I blamed not only myself, but Derrick as well for losing our baby.

Chapter Eighteen

Knock! Knock!

"Yes!"

"Passion, I'm coming in!" Derrick said.

"Derrick, I just really wish you wouldn't!" It was like I didn't say anything. Derrick came in our room and laid on the bed with me. He didn't say anything. He just looked at me and I at him without saying a word. We both just kept staring at each other until I noticed a tear forming in his eyes. Unfortunately, the caring side of me moved my hand to wipe away his tears. This small notion of care was all he needed. He moved closely to me and put his arm across me. Something inside of me was tired of fussing and fighting so I gave in. We were both showing each other what we so desperately needed; a gesture of care. We found ourselves wrapped in one another's arms as we wept quietly. No words, no anger, this felt like he loved me through it all. Derrick and I finally slept in the same bed after all this time, and it felt good.

"Ring, Ring!" Is what I heard in my ear as I rolled over and unwrapped myself from Derrick's grasp.

"Hello!" My voice raspy from fatigue.

"Hello, is this Mrs. Wilson?" The voice asked.

"Yes, it is! Who is this?"

"Mrs. Wilson, this is Nurse Johnson from Dr. Henderson's office. The test results came back, are you and your husband available to come into the office at 10?"

"Hold on ma'am. Derrick the results are back, and they want us to come in at 10. Is that good with you?" I asked.

"Yes, that's fine!" Derrick whispered."

"Ma'am, that's fine. We will be there."

"Ok, great! See you all then."

I hung up the phone and sat up in the bed. Fear had come over my whole body. I was afraid of the results. Could I be HIV positive and if so, what do I expect? I've heard stories of how people lose weight and look so sick, but the real question is, how long will I live?

"My God! This can't be happening!" I yelled.

"Passion let's think positive! I'm so sorry babe!" Derrick uttered out.

Derrick sat up next to me in the bed as we both stared into space.

"There is no need to just keep sitting here Derrick. It's already eight thirty. Let's get up and get ready."

He didn't say a word as we went into separate bathrooms to prepare for this dreaded day. While brushing my teeth and cleansing my face, I stared into the mirror. My fears were playing tug of war inside my mind. I could feel my thoughts pulling at my emotions and the feelings within my heart. I felt like I did as a child playing the game. I would always be on the team that lost; weakest people at the front when they should have been at the back. They would always let go first. Thinking this way made my fears pull harder on my feelings. Will I let go first because I'm so weak now? It's one thing after another. Can I be a wife of noble character like stated in the bible? Will Derrick still think I'm worth more than rubies? If it's determined, we both are HIV positive will we have full confidence and lack nothing in each other? Only time will tell. So as for today, the clock will start to tick a bit louder. As I continued to get dressed, I tried to refrain from looking in my mirror of fears. I had to be real with myself. Will I win this tug of war that has just escalated in our lives? I've got to grab the ropes I know that will help me to overcome the tugs of fear and continue my journey in life. Well, enough of this Passion!" I said to myself, put on the armor within you and go to war! I kept re-playing this in my mind as I finished getting dressed. "Derrick are you ready?" I yelled in the other room.

"Yes!" He stated as he walked in the hallway. "Let's go."

"Derrick, I'm so scared! I don't think I can drive. My focus is off. Can you please drive?"

"Yes, Passion. I think I can."

We locked up the house and entered our family car, a black Cadillac CTS. We usually only drove it on Sundays or for road trips, but since Derrick's car was at the police station and he didn't want to drive my car, family car it is. Derrick proceeded to back out the garage and before pulling onto the road he looked all around. Twice.

"Derrick there are no cars coming. What are you looking around for?" I asked.

"Just checking the surroundings." He said.

I take it that he is being very observant now since all this has occurred. Derrick backed up and drove carefully up the road. When we came to the main highway that would take us to the doctor's office, I noticed Derrick staring over into the parking lot of a convenience store.

"Do you see something of interest at the store?" I asked.

"Huh!" He responded.

"You have the right of way and you still sitting her at the light."

"Oh, I was in deep thought!" He said.

"Oh, ok! I thought you were looking at something."

Derrick turned right and continued to the doctor's office. Once we arrived, he got out first and came and opened my door. I got out and we walked into the office. Derrick signed us in, and we sat down to wait our turn to be seen. Finally, the nurse called our names, and we entered one of the rooms in the back. She explained to us that the doctor would be in momentarily. The door opened and in walked Dr. Henderson.

"Hello, Mr. and Mrs. Wilson! How are you all today?"

Derrick responded, "We seem to be doing ok right now."

"Well, I'm not going to beat around the bush with you two, you have been through enough within the last two days as it is. So, I'm going to start with some good news, Mrs. Wilson your results are negative. Now, that doesn't mean that they might not come back later and test positive, but for now, you seem to be ok. I would however, like for you to get tested in about six months from today. Now, Mr. Wilson your results remained the same. You tested positive once again. So, I would like to start you on treatment as soon as possible. I would like to refer you to a specialist so they can assist with your medication and treatment regime. We also can refer you to courses and support groups to help you better understand and cope with your diagnosis. I know that most people hear HIV and think death, but that is not the case in most instances. I have patience who are living wonderful lives with HIV. Some have even had children and have lived over twenty years after their diagnosis. I will have the nurse provide some pamphlets today and all the numbers you will need. I must inform you that we do have to report this to the state so they will reach out to you as well. I hope I have explained this in a manner you can understand. I know this isn't what you wanted to hear, but it is your reality now. How you live it out is solely on you. Just know we are here to assist you in any way we possibly can. Do you all have any questions for me?" He asked.

With tears streaming down my face, I asked the doctor, "So, is it safe for me to continue any type of sexual relations with my husband? Or does it even matter?"

"Well, it does matter. Because currently you are negative. Therefore, I would say practice safe sex."

"Passion, is that all you are worried about, is you? Did you just fucking hear the doctor? He said I'm positive. So, you have no remorse or concern about what I must be feeling right now? Ok, I get it, you may think I deserve this, because of me cheating. Damn Passion! Can you think of me for once?" Derrick yelled, with tears flowing.

"Derrick, yes! I am thinking of you, I know we have some big decisions to make too. There is an old saying though, don't cry over spilled milk. See, babe! Our reality now is that the milk has spilled, and we can't retrieve it. All we can do now is try and soak some of it up with the towels and napkins of our lives. Last night laying in the bed next to you I finally figured out I've been crying over things I can't change. So, I must soak up the lesson God is giving use and move on. Yes, I can divorce you and go on, but with this monkey of HIV floating around our heads, why swing around in the world knowing I could cause someone else's milk to spill? Yes, you are contaminated now, but the man I know and grew to love will soak his spills up with the strongest towel he possesses. Now figure out what that towel is, Derrick! We can't think about anything else right now, but what the doctor is offering us and how we are going to apply it to our lives." I shared as I cried.

"Mrs. Wilson I couldn't have said it better." The doctor stated.

"I hear you Passion. So, does this mean you're staying with me? Or is this just another way of you trying to make me feel guilty?" Derrick asked.

"Derrick! Let me put it to you this way. It's been said that when hunters go hunting, they have hunting dogs to sniff out the prey, rifles to kill them, knives to skin them, ropes to hang them or tie the animals together. This is an enjoyable sport for some of them. See, you been hunting for years. You were hunting for women and got caught two days ago by your fellow hunters. Now the very ropes you once used to hang females, has you tied up. You are now bound with an illness that won't let you go. Now you feel as though you were shot in more ways than one, and that's true, but don't try and act like the hunter who never enjoyed the sport. That would be me! See, I share your feelings babe. Trust me I really do. I didn't enjoy the sport of hunting, I stayed home and left that to you. Mostly, because I knew that I once was your prey and I got hung on a wall. I remembered what I learned from you when you first cheated. Remember that? The time you brought home the disease. My mother used to always say that, "The same trap you set for another could be the trap you set for yourself." It's just now, you set the trap for the both of us. So, yes, I'm staying in this marriage. You won't get off that easy! Now, you think about me too. I'm now trapped in a life that I didn't set or plan for myself either!" I guess it really was a cliché.

MEET THE AUTHOR

Pamela Buchanan can usually be found reading a romance novel with relatability to her life. She also enjoys reading the Holy Bible that brings structure in her everyday living. Because of her enjoyment of reading and writing a novel that others could relate to was always on her bucket list, and eventually,

with *Destruction of True Friendships* it became a reality. How many times in life do people have friendships that destruct and leave us distraught? After being distraught from so many untrue friendships, Pamela found her purpose in life by writing, working for nonprofits organizations and working as a college Admissions Coordinator. These helped in her healing process and allowed new friendships to form. She now knows the real meaning of true friendships. She is the youngest of seven children, but in reality the oldest in statue. Pamela often gives her mother, Mildred Goodall, great gratitude for being a single parent. She is also very thankful for the friendship she acquired with Laquita Davis, who played a great part in her being an author. Pamela currently resides in the state of Texas and is excitedly working on become an inspiring author. She is currently writing her second book titled "Trapped."

www.ingramcontent.com/pod-product-compliance
Lightning Source LLC
Chambersburg PA
CBHW031207260626
47169CB00004B/1280